Sydney Wakefield:
Into the Faraway

ISBN 978-1-387-56921-2

Montage Books for Children
Dallas, Texas

Cover art ©2006 Kevin Lory Mote
Third U.S. Edition

Printed in the United States of America

SYDNEY WAKEFIELD: INTO THE FARAWAY

by
Kimberly J. Smith

MONTAGE BOOKS FOR CHILDREN | DALLAS

For Harrison
and Benjamin.
Your love of a good story
and your encouragement
constantly inspire me
to keep writing.

For Steven.
Your support
and love made
this book possible.

And, of course,
For Arthur!

PART ONE

Sydney gasped. That was her name, carved elegantly into the stone wall of the dank and dripping cell.

Sydney Wakefield. Like it had been there for centuries.

"Do you see?" the knight whispered, his grime-smudged face beaming with hope. "You are the one who will free King Arthur, and all of Avalon!"

SYDNEY WAKEFIELD
AND THE DOORWAY TO AVALON

CHAPTER 1

I totally screwed up.

I fell asleep. How did I let that happen? I never did that. Not on these nights, anyway.

Just moments ago, I was waiting for midnight—that glorious second at 12 o'clock and zero seconds AM where I let myself read the newest book. Except now the morning sun beamed through my window. That didn't happen at midnight. What was going on?

"Let's go, young man, or you'll have to take the tube to school." My head swiveled to find Mom standing next to my bed, scowling down at me. A white toothbrush poked out of her mouth. She scrubbed violently a couple of times before removing it to talk.

"I can't be late today," she warned through the toothpaste. She jabbed the toothbrush at the book lying open across my chest. "How was it?"

I launched myself into a sitting position and snatched up the book. Horrified, I slammed it shut. No! This wasn't possible!

With a glance at the clock I realized school started in half an hour. I kicked back the sheets, banged the book against my forehead twice—a stupid thing to do because it hurt—and wailed like an old dog abandoned in the backyard.

Mom backed away as I scramble out of bed. "Henderson, my goodness! What's wrong?"

I snatched the ugly school uniform off the back of my desk chair. Back in Texas I hadn't worn a uniform, but I was in London now. Things were different here. Don't get me wrong, I loved the difference. I just hated the uniform. It was tight and uncomfortable. And I hated having to wear a tie.

"I fell asleep!" I growled. "I didn't finish the book!"

Yanking on the navy slacks, I pulled on the light blue shirt, stuffed the striped tie into my jacket pocket, and ran a hand over my head. I didn't need a mirror to know I had total bed head because I always had bed head: wacky brown strands poking up all over like I was some psychotic hedgehog. On days that I cared, I made it behave by taking a brush to it, but today I definitely didn't care.

"Oh honey. I know you wanted to finish it the same way you did the others, but—"

"Mom, you know I read them all the same way. It's my thing!" I froze. Wait, what if ... I threw her one of my most winning looks, the one where I look most like my dad. "Would it be okay if I stayed home and—"

Mom's eyes shrunk to slits and she pointed her foamy toothbrush at me. "You are not skipping school." Maybe "the dad look" wasn't such a great idea. He wasn't exactly high on her list anymore. "Oh, HG," she sighed, "I don't understand why this ritual always has to take place at midnight! It's amazing you've never fallen asleep before!" She rolled her eyes. "I've got to spit."

"Mo-om," I whined, hating how my voice sounded. "It's my thing!"

"Yes, you said that already."

"But I've never fallen asleep before, I don't know what happened this time! Please! I can't go to school without knowing what happens!"

Mom shrugged, as if the whole thing was so far beyond her she couldn't possibly think of a response, and headed for her bathroom to finish brushing her teeth. Mom didn't understand anything, including me, her only son. Now, her job ... she got that. Probably why she spent more time working than with my sister and me.

I yanked the bed covers up to the headboard and tossed my pillows on top, then ducked into the small bathroom between my room and Claire's to give my own teeth a short brush—just enough to kill the morning breath. Stuffing the unfinished book in my backpack, I rushed downstairs, snagged a cereal bar and a bottle of cranberry juice, and raced out the front door. I actually remembered to lock it behind me so Mom wouldn't yell at me for that, too.

She waited with Claire in the Renault with the engine running. I hopped in the back seat. "You're going to be late." Mom predicted with a shake of her head as if I'd planned this or something.

"Mom, don't you think it's kind of lame that HG totally worships some girl who only exists in a book?" Claire threw the comment over her shoulder like it was salt she'd spilled and she needed good luck. She wore her long, blonde hair in a fancy braid that I had to admit was pretty impressive.

"Can it, Claire," Mom snapped, saving my sister from one of my razor-sharp comebacks. Claire huffed, totally annoyed as usual.

Claire had begged to go to ASL, the American School of London, but Mom said no. She wanted us to be "immersed in the British culture." I was all for that, even before I became a Sydney Wakefield fan. Claire has been mad about it ever since. I didn't understand why, she was just as popular in London as she ever was back in Dallas. Even though we went to different schools, I'd heard enough from the younger brothers and sisters of Claire's classmates to know the girl ruled the halls. Colin couldn't speak a word when she was around, he'd turn all red and sweaty. Not that he had a chance with her. Claire went through guys like breath mints, although the most recent—some lacrosse player named Ian—had stuck for the last few weeks. I heard her talking to him on the phone late at night, all giggles and sighs. Gag.

I buckled up and slumped against the door. Even Claire was no distraction from my epic screw up. Double screw up, actually. Not finishing the book was a problem, yes, but so was being late for the first day of seventh year. They didn't look kindly upon that kind of thing at Dowd Secondary School.

Three years ago, after my mom and dad split up, Mom, Claire, and I moved to London. You might think I wouldn't like being "dragged across the pond," as Dad put it, but you'd be wrong. He didn't seem too broken up about it, but maybe that had something to do with his new girlfriend, Sheri, with an "I." Sure, I'd miss Dad and my best friends Drew and Ethan but, honestly, school in Dallas was complete torture.

Most kids at "The Dub"—a.k.a. George W. Bush Elementary—didn't even know I existed. The ones who did went out of their way to let me know they thought I was a total loser. Not that they actually did anything to me; I mean, I never got beat up or had my head shoved into a toilet or anything like that. But taking their lame digs with a smile stunk like sweaty week-old gym socks left in a backpack.

So what if my friends and I liked reading more than playing football? Did every boy on the planet have to be able to take a tackle or throw a perfect spiral to fit in? It sure seemed that way, especially in Texas. Sure,

I played hoops in my driveway sometimes, but unless you played competitively it didn't make a blip on your coolness meter.

For me, a new school in a new country meant a new chance to build a reputation that didn't include the word "loser" in it. Not that I wasn't nervous about the whole moving thing, I mean, who wouldn't be? But the first time I stepped into our flat in Chelsea, I felt this instant sense of relief. And my bedroom, it was like I'd already slept there every night of my life already. I felt at home.

The room was nothing like my room back in Dallas. Our new flat was in a building that was way older than anything I'd ever lived in before. My bedroom walls were painted dark purple, a shade my mom called "eggplant." I just called it wicked cool.

My room had this big window with a padded window seat and a view overlooking Sloane Gardens, the tiny little park behind our building. The flat was full of cool things like that—hidden nooks and crannies, even a whole attic above my sister's room that you could only get to through a hidden panel that slid back.

So, I wasn't too surprised to find the secret compartment in the back of my closet. The tiny wooden door in the floor had a metal loop for a handle, but no matter how hard I pulled it, it wouldn't budge. It took me a few days, but with the help of a butter knife I finally got it open. Inside the wooden compartment were some old photographs, letters, a necklace, a funky mood ring, and a chunk of rock about the size of a robin's egg. It looked like some kid had stashed it there years ago and just forgot about it. I took everything out of the compartment and kept it in a shoebox on my closet shelf. Except for the rock. There was something about it that I liked. It was just a plain old rock with flecks of red, but I liked the way it fit in my palm. I liked how it felt when I held it. Like I was holding something old and important. And a little magical.

That was just my imagination, of course. I had a darn good one. It got me in trouble all the time.

But all that cool stuff about our flat didn't even begin to compare with the coolest fun fact of all: our flat is that it's the same flat where Fern Caldwell, my favorite author, grew up. Fern Caldwell wrote the most amazing books on the face of the planet: the Sydney Wakefield books.

"Henderson, did you get your homework done?" Mom asked, as she zoomed into Sloane Street traffic.

"Yes, ma'am."

I pulled the book from my backpack. I'd read about two sentences before Claire started in on Mom. "Mo-ther! You're being totally unreasonable. I don't want to go to university here. Dad already said he'd pay for college in Texas, so holding tuition over my head isn't going to work." Claire paused, then added: "You treat me like such a baby. I'm seventeen, you know."

"Believe me, Claire, I am extremely aware of your age," Mom grumbled, stomping on the brake. London traffic was worse than Dallas, which was saying something. Driving almost always made her swear, but today she controlled herself and didn't even honk.

I tried to ignore their conversation and concentrate on the book, but my eyes wouldn't focus. I was so tired—and my mind kept detouring to Fern Caldwell.

By the time I reached the end of the first chapter of the first book, Sydney Wakefield and the Doorway to Avalon, I was already a huge Fern Caldwell fan. The book had everything I loved: knights, a shadow realm, King Arthur, and the evil Morgan le Fay. But Sydney Wakefield wasn't just another spin on the King Arthur story. They had something no other Arthur story could: Sydney. She was one of the coolest literary heroes ever, in my opinion. Smart, brave, and she totally kicked butt.

I'd heard about Doorway to Avalon from a saleslady at Foyles bookstore way before any of the real buzz started, and I gave it a try. Nobody had really heard of it then, making me and my friend Colin (who I immediately talked into reading it) original fans. Nobody could call us bandwagon hoppers.

It didn't take long before that first book was all anyone talked about. A total Phenom.

Fourteen years old, Sydney Wakefield lived in Glastonbury, a quaint town out in the southwest English countryside. She was lucky enough to discover a magical doorway into the mythical world of Avalon. In Fern Caldwell's books, Avalon was a shadow realm created by Morgan le Fay to hold King Arthur prisoner. If you know anything about the King Arthur legends, then you know that they all say Morgan sailed Arthur to Avalon after that last horrible battle he fought with Modred. Supposedly, she wanted to heal Arthur so he could return someday and properly rule England. The once and future King, and all that. But in the Sydney Wakefield books, that part of the story is just something Morgan le Fay made up and spread around the world as a cover, so that no one would know her true goal was to keep Arthur from ever taking the throne.

When Morgan cast her evil spell, creating the shadow realm, doubles of all the people living in Camelot at that moment were trapped in Avalon. Basically, she'd cursed them to exist in an out-of-place/out-of-time dimension where Morgan's son Modred rules as King. Early on in that first book, Sydney ends up trapped in the shadow realm. There she meets a Knight of the Round Table: Sir Bedivere. He believes Sydney's arrival was predicted in Merlin's prophesy—making her the one destined to save Arthur. Bedivere spends a lot of that first book trying to convince Sydney it's true.

The book was a cliffhanger, but I loved that because it meant the story would go on. I just didn't like having to wait a year for the next one.

The next two books in the series were out: Sydney Wakefield: The Secret of the Tor and Sydney Wakefield: The Sword Hunters—that was the book I meant to finish last night. At midnight.

It was my thing.

I'm a fast reader and can easily blaze through a book in a couple of days, but I prided myself on making each Sydney Wakefield book last all the way through the summer holiday. I broke down the chapters and allowed myself just enough to read that last chapter right before school began. I know some kids read the books as fast as possible, some staying up all that first night until they were finished. Not me.

Sometimes I read the same three chapters over and over until it was time to read the next one. There was one section of Secret of the Tor I'd read ten times. But when it came to the last chapter, it had to be read the night before the first day of school, at midnight, under the bedcovers, and by flashlight. There was just something special about that. I'd done that with the first book and when it came to the second, I decided to make it a ritual. It had been my plan to finish Sword Hunters that way, too.

Colin had finished his copy weeks ago, but had kept mum about everything; hadn't let even one juicy plot point slip. "Wouldn't want to ruin it for you, mate," he'd said, exchanging a knowing look with Libby, the third of our trio at school. Sometimes it bugged me that Colin and Libby knew what happened before I did, and had Sydney Wakefield secrets from me, but not enough to break the ritual.

Finally, after weeks of stringing myself along this summer, the time had come to read the last chapter. To find out what was going to happen with Bedivere and Sydney.

And I'd fallen asleep.

What was wrong with me?

The car jerked to a stop. I looked up and discovered we'd arrived at school. "Okay, sweetie. Here we are," Mom said, her voice kind but firm. She glanced in the rearview mirror and raised an eyebrow at me.

With a sigh, I snapped the book shut. I hadn't read a word.

Mom turned in the seat and gave me a sympathetic smile. "You'll have time to read at school I'm sure. Have a great day! Learn lots!"

I tried to smile but failed. Grabbing my stuff, I slunk out of the car, ignoring Claire who ignored me back with a pout as I slammed the door.

Colin and Libby waited on the big front stone steps. Dowd Secondary was one of those ancient London buildings in which children had been schooled since the dark ages. Or at least a few hundred years. On the outside, it looked like a gothic old castle, but the interior had been updated so it looked pretty much like any school: tile floors, glass doors, and fluorescent lights that fed on your soul.

I approached my friends sullenly, each step ached with disappointment. It wasn't just that I didn't know how Sword Hunters ended, although it was rather embarrassing to return to school without knowing the big cliffhanger. There was always a cliffhanger. After all, I was the biggest Sydney Wakefield fan in the entire school. That wasn't even self-proclaimed; I'd actually been voted that in last year's "best of" for the yearbook.

But I'd broken tradition. Screwed up the ritual. This was my thing and I'd blown it.

Colin and Libby watched me approach, their expressions anxious. Colin's white-blond hair looked freshly trimmed: his holiday curls gone, making him look even taller and thinner than usual. On the other end of the height spectrum was Libby, a girl my grandmother would have called a "little wisp o' a thing." Grandma loved that phrase, course she'd liked using it to describe me, but that was before my growth spurt. Libby had deep, blue eyes and thick golden hair, which she wore pulled back from her face in a ponytail of ringlets. She had a pixie-ish look to her, like she'd just stepped out of a storybook.

I tried to prevent any spoilers as I approached. "Before you say anything," I held up one hand, "I didn't finish Sword Hunters last night. I … fell asleep. It's ridiculous, I know. Me, of all people! But it happened. So, I still have a chapter to go. I'll try to sneak a read in Lit. Then we can discuss it all at lunch."

Colin and Libby exchanged a silent shocked look. "Henderson, wait, you don't know?" Colin's eyes went all misty. Whoa, hold on. This was more than just being stunned that I fell asleep. I'd never seen Colin cry before. Something else was wrong.

"Don't I know what?" I asked, the hairs on the back of my neck standing up in warning. I slipped my hand into my pocket and wrapped my fingers around the rock, nervously turning it over and over.

"You didn't catch the news this morning?" Colin continued in his smooth London accent.

My heartbeat sped up even more. "No, I didn't see the news! I'm a kid, I don't watch the news! What happened?"

They exchanged that look again, and then Libby lost it. She cried into her hands and wouldn't look at me. That was the final straw. "What is going on?" I yelled.

Colin's freckles stood out against his milky cheeks so much it looked like someone had dotted them on with a felt tip pen. "It's Fern Caldwell," he stammered. "You'd better sit down, mate."

My knees felt like Jell-O cubes as I lowered myself onto the stone bench at the top of the steps. The bell rang, but I didn't care. That's when I realized that scads of kids weren't going inside yet either. They huddled in groups all over the front yard, talking in wide-eyed whispers, some with hands over their mouths like Libby, some weeping openly. A few teachers stood among them, patting backs and talking in a way that teachers only did when something tragic had happened. My stomach clenched as if someone had kicked me in the belly.

"Tell. Me. Now!"

Libby burst out a sob. "Oh, Henderson. Fern Caldwell died last night!"

Do you know how it feels when you jump into a swimming pool in the spring, before the water has warmed up? I did because, back when we lived in Dallas, I fell into our backyard pool one March and let me tell you it was way cold. Like falling into a pit of cold silence. Then comes the rush of freezing shock. Your heart stops beating for a moment. You want to breathe but you can't make your lungs work, and you shouldn't of course, because if you suck in a breath, it's going to be all water, and then that's all she wrote. If you're lucky, like I was, you get your wits about you. You paddle for the surface where hands can drag you from the icy water, where you can gulp in freezing air.

The moment I found out about Fern Caldwell felt just like that. Except this time, it ended in darkness.

When I opened my eyes the first time, I saw blurry versions of Colin and Libby hovering over me. Their mouths moved, but all I heard was this funky humming sound. A dark circle flooded the edges of my vision and moved inward until there was just blackness again.

The next time I opened my eyes, I was in the nurse's office.

"There you are, lovey," Miss Flannigan cooed, dark eyes wide behind thick, cat's-eye glasses. "You feelin' a bit better there?" Miss Flannigan always looked like she'd ended up in the wrong decade somehow, missing the present by about fifty years.

"How'd I get in here?" I whispered. My head pounded and my body felt stuffed with cotton.

"You had a bit of a fall out there at the entry I'm afraid. Knocked your noggin a bit, you did." She smiled and patted my hand. "Just rest for a spell now, dear one." She started to get up, then thought of something. "Oh yes, Colin said you'd be wanting this."

She slipped my rock into my hand. Tears burned as I folded my fingers around it. I stared up at the paneled ceiling and florescent lights as they ran from my eyes. The plastic light cover was specked with the bodies of dead bugs.

"Fern Caldwell," I whispered. "She's dead."

Miss Flannigan sighed deeply. "Yes, apparently that's true. Such a tragic thing, isn't it?"

"But how? Why?" I sobbed, letting the sadness out. "She can't be. She just can't be!"

"Shhhhh now …" Miss Flannigan stroked my hair, patting my arm. "It's a horrible thing but it'll be all right. Just breathe, dearie."

No, everything was not going to be all right. My favorite author in the whole world was gone. Just, gone! There would never be another Sydney Wakefield book. Ever! The story would never be finished and a wonderful author's creations would just stop.

I felt like such a baby, crying there in the nurse's office. But I couldn't help it. I cried for Sydney, for King Arthur, for Bedivere, for this horrible ending. But mostly, I cried for Fern Caldwell, whose own story was cut short.

That's when Mom walked in. Flannigan had called her, of course. Amazingly, Mom was great about the whole thing. She hugged me for a long time, then took me home. She took the rest of the day off work and just sat with me. She watched me sleep, listened to me cry, hugged me and held my hand. I don't know if she actually understood why I was so upset, but she acted like it. She was so great that day.

After school, Colin and Libby came by to visit and brought me my homework and some chocolate, which helped me feel better. The chocolate, not the homework. Homework on the first day? And a first day with such horrible news? So wrong.

Gloomy old London felt cloaked in sadness. Rain started around lunch, and as the sun went down the tree branches drooped, heavy with rainy tears. The streetlamp lights seemed dimmer than usual and the rain-soaked streets sighed with each passing car.

After dinner, Mom turned on the TV so we could watch the news. Fern Caldwell's death was the lead story. News crews swarmed over Glastonbury. Home to both Sydney Wakefield and Fern Caldwell, the little town was the heart of her stories. Supposedly, hundreds of years ago, some monks found the grave of King Arthur buried where the Glastonbury Abbey now stood. Some say a castle called Camelot wasn't far from there.

The reporter talked about how Glastonbury was such a hotbed of King Arthur lore. I wondered if it made Mom think about Aunt Maggie. She didn't talk about her little sister much, but Claire and I knew Maggie had run away from home after she graduated from college. Run away to Glastonbury.

This happened before both Claire and I were born, but we both knew the story. When Mom first sprung it on us that we were moving to London, Claire asked if we would be able to visit Aunt Maggie. Mom said

Maggie didn't consider us family anymore. We could tell talking about Maggie upset her, so we dropped it.

As I watched the crowds of people gathering outside Fern Caldwell's house, I couldn't help but wonder if Aunt Maggie was there. I wondered if Mom thought the same thing.

The reporter had a gleam of hungry sadness in her eye as she explained that Fern had died in her sleep. Fern's agent, a man named Stanley Doonesbury, had driven out to Glastonbury from London when Fern didn't show up for a meeting with her publisher and he wasn't able to reach her by phone. The reporter said authorities suspected Fern had a heart attack, but were awaiting post mortem results.

"What's post mortem?" I asked.

"An autopsy. To find out exactly how she died," Mom answered dully.

"Wasn't she pretty young to have a heart attack?" I asked.

"That's why they're doing the autopsy." Mom gave me a sad smile.

The news report showed Stanley Doonesbury, who looked pretty shook up. He said the publishing world had lost one of its greatest contributors.

No kidding, I thought. And tears burned behind my eyes again.

I lay in my bed that night, listening to the rain's soothing rhythm. I was so tired, but my mind wouldn't shut down; wouldn't let me forget what happened. Finally, my swollen eyes grew heavy. I just wanted to escape into sleep. To forget everything. As I felt myself finally drifting off, my eyes popped open as with a jolt of adrenaline shot through my veins.

Someone was in my room.

Someone was standing beside my bed.

And that someone was Fern Caldwell.

Bedivere pushed Sydney through a small doorway in a back section of the castle's kitchen. Someone stood across the torch-lit room, huddled near a table against the back wall. Sydney could barely see her in the dim light.

The figure took a step toward them. It was Isabelle, the girl who had snuck food into Sydney's dungeon cell. "You did it," Isabelle whispered, her wide eyes sparkling with hope. "You found the key!"

Bedivere held a finger to his lips as the sound of running feet echoed in the hallway outside. Guards. Headed toward the dungeon. Bedivere gritted his teeth. "Our escape will soon be known," he warned. "We must leave the castle. Isabelle, you know what must be done."

SYDNEY WAKEFIELD
AND THE DOORWAY TO AVALON

CHAPTER 2

The Fern Caldwell book signing happened at the beginning of the summer holiday. It was the week right after the release of Sword Hunters and I was completely chuffed (as my Brit friends say) about seeing her in real life. I was also so nervous I didn't sleep a wink the night before, and we had to get up super early for a good spot in line.

It wasn't early enough, though. Some crazy fools slept on the sidewalk outside of Foyles bookstore all night to be first in line to see her. And even though we got to the bookstore before sun-up, Colin, Libby, and I waited for five hours before we even got through the front door. The line inside snaked through the store for another hour. But honestly, I would have waited all day if I had to. I'd never fanboyed out over an author like I had over Fern Caldwell. I'd seen her in magazines and on TV before, of course, but it wasn't the same as meeting her in person. She was one of the most famous authors on the planet, at least when it came to books for kids. She was worth billions, and could probably afford to live in a castle or something, but she lived in the same old flat in Glastonbury where she'd lived back before she was famous. I thought that was kind of cool, how she tried to be so normal and everything. Apparently, people in Glastonbury were cool about leaving her alone—nobody mobbed her on the streets or anything, at least according to the articles I'd read online about her.

Things were different when she came to London.

By time we neared the front of the line, Colin, Libby, and I were tired, sweaty, and hungry. But none of that mattered as I got my first glance of the author to whom I'd pledged my reading life. She was writing in someone's book, so I could only see the part in her wavy dark brown hair, but even that made my heart race.

I shifted my weight from one foot to the next, bouncing up and down to keep my excitement from bubbling over, thinking about an interview I'd seen with Fern on the news not long after Doorway to Avalon started really taking off. It wasn't about her book, actually, but part of a news report about a girl in Glastonbury who had maybe been kidnapped. She was a neighbor of Fern's, who was highly involved in her search. Standing there in line, I couldn't remember whether the police had ever found that girl—it seemed like months passed and there was no new news—but I'd hadn't forgotten her name.

It was Sydney.

Fern had named the character in her book for the girl. The Glastonbury police suspected she'd been kidnapped, but nobody tried to get a ransom or anything. If she'd turned up it would have been big news, and I couldn't imagine I could have missed it. But I wasn't sure.

I brushed away the memory. This wasn't some TV news report. This was the real thing. And it was almost my turn.

Fern was thirty-three years old, but she looked so much younger. Her chocolate-colored hair fell in soft waves over the tops of her shoulders and her deep purple blouse had sort of a medieval look with its flowing, loose collar and billowy sleeves. Around her neck hung a thin piece of leather with a small stone pendant. It was rough, not polished like most necklace stones. I stuck my hand in my pocket, running my thumb along the rough surface of my lucky stone.

With small, quick scratches, Fern finished scribbling her signature in Colin's book and glanced up at him with deep blue eyes that reminded me of the night sky right before morning. I took my hand out of my pocket and nudged the googly-eyed idiot out of the way.

Finally, Fern Caldwell turned her eyes my way. "And what would your name be, my young friend?" she asked in a smooth English accent that felt like slipping a silk hat over your ears. I swear I saw a flicker of recognition in her eyes, like when you see someone you've met a long time before but can't quite remember where or when.

"Henderson Green," I stammered, and handed her my copies of her first two books I'd brought from home.

"Henderson Green …" she said, taking them from me with a pause like she needed to let my name sink in before writing it on the page.

Colin coughed and gave me a hard look. He wanted me to tell her about my flat. He'd been talking about it all morning, insisting that I had to say something about it. How could I let a chance like this go by?

I took a deep breath and just started talking, something that was easier once she dropped her gaze to my book and started signing. Oxygen made it into my lungs better when she wasn't looking right at me.

"Um, excuse me, Ms. Caldwell?"

"Oh, no, no, no. You must call me Fern."

"Oh. Right, okay. Fern. Well, here's something crazy. You won't believe this, but you used to live in my flat."

She didn't miss a beat, just finished signing the new book and snapped it shut before looking up at me without the surprise I had expected to see. "Do you mean the flat at Sloane Gardens?"

"Yeah!"

Her eyebrows raised and a big grin spread across her face. "You live there, do you?" she said. "How extraordinary! And an American at that."

I nodded. "It is extraordinary." I said the word just like she did, with an accent that made it come out "ex-TRO-dinry." I'm sure I sounded like an idiot.

Fern finished signing the other books I'd brought from home and handed them back to me. I clutched them to my chest.

"Come by and visit any time." The words were out of my mouth before I could think. "That is, if you'd like to, you know, see the place again."

What a dork. Seriously. Colin should have slapped me.

But Fern just smiled and cocked her head as if surprised by the invitation, but not uncomfortable or anything. "Well! I certainly appreciate that. Henderson Green." She leaned forward, her elbows on the table and stage-whispered. "Think that'd be all right with your mum?"

"She'd love it!" I said and suddenly words started coming out of my mouth. "Hey, 'member that girl you were looking for back in Glastonbury, the real Sydney—did anyone ever find her?"

Fern's smile disappeared in an instant. Leave it to me to screw everything up. The King of Killjoy, that's me. "No, I'm afraid not." Colin, Libby, and the other lady behind the desk with Fern helping with the books all stared at me like I'd just told Fern Caldwell she had bad breath or something. I guess what I'd said was worse. My insides went icy.

"Oh, gosh, I—I'm so sorry. Never mind."

Fern shook her head. "No, it's fine." Fern looked so sad that I decided to bail before I messed things up any further.

"Thanks. For the autograph, I mean. Can't wait for the fourth book." That seemed like the right thing to say.

"You'll have to, at least until next holiday." She seemed to shake off the sadness with a wink, before turning her attention to the next devoted fan.

Colin and I moved to the side as we waited for Libby, who was a few people back in the line with her cousin, Anita Carl. I flipped open the cover of Sword Hunters to see what Fern Caldwell had written next to her signature.

> *To Henderson Green,*
> *always remember that reading can open any*
> *doorway!*
> > *Best,*
> > *Fern Caldwell*

I beamed. It was the perfect addition to the Sydney Wakefield display in my bedroom.

The Tor rose up to greet them as they neared Glastonbury. The sound of faraway bells stirred the morning air. Sydney stared at the crest of the tall hill, feeling her blood turn cold. "Wait. Where is St. Michael's?" she asked. Instead of the ruins of the singular tower rising from the grass, an enormous church perched atop the Tor.

Bedivere followed her gaze. "St. Michaels's? No, St. Joseph's. It was built by the abbey monks years ago to protect their most precious treasures. One of which is an entrance to the sacred tunnels beneath the Tor. I believe that is where Morgan hid Excalibur."

Isabelle drew up short, hand raised. Following her lead, they ducked behind a copse of bushy growth. Her eyes flashed a warning in the morning twilight. Stay quiet!

Sydney held her breath as her heartbeat quickened in time with the frantic thump of approaching hoof beats.

SYDNEY WAKEFIELD
AND THE SECRET OF THE TOR

CHAPTER 3

When word first got around school that I lived in the flat where Fern Caldwell grew up, my popularity level spiked. All the kids in the neighborhood wanted to come over and see the flat. I set up a corner of my room with a bookcase that held action figures of Sydney and Sir Bedivere (mint-in-the-box, of course), some framed pictures of Fern Caldwell that I'd cut out of magazines, and my first editions of the Sydney Wakefield books.

To complete the effect, I'd hung a theater banner from the first Sydney Wakefield movie on the wall behind my bed. I wished I had a poster from Secret of the Tor too, but by time that movie came out, Sydney Wakefield items were hard to come by. I considered myself pretty smart to snag that first one: I saw one going for $500 on eBay once, no joke.

The main part of banner over my bed was a close-up of Tara Benjamin, the girl who played Sydney Wakefield in the movies. The Sword Hunters movie was supposed to come out this Christmas, and the fourth and final untitled book in the series was due out next summer.

At least, that had been the plan.

All this was on my mind as I lay in my bed that horrible rainy night after Fern died, hoping and praying that Fern had finished the fourth book before … what happened had happened. Then maybe Sydney's story wouldn't be unfinished after all. I felt horrible thinking that, because obviously Fern's life was over and that was tons sadder than not finish a book.

But when I saw that ghost standing at the foot of my bed, a little spark of something took life. And when she started talking to me, it didn't take long to figure out that the story wasn't over. Not by a long shot. And for me, it was just beginning.

When I realized my favorite author was standing beside my bed (my favorite recently deceased author), I didn't scream, which is what you might think you'd do if you saw a real, honest-to-goodness ghost. Nope. Not me. But only because I couldn't breathe.

It's difficult to scream without breathing.

This was a good thing, actually, because if I had screamed, Mom would have come running and things might not have turned out the way they did.

'I must be dreaming,' I thought.

"You aren't dreaming, Henderson Green," Fern said in her velvety soft accent. "I'm really here. And you're quite awake."

The room swam dangerously, darkness ebbing and flowing in my vision as if I was stuck in some river of goo. It felt as if my bed tilted, trying to throw me onto the floor. Was I was going to pass out again and make it a pass-out hat trick, like in soccer when you score three goals? Could you pass out if you were already lying down? What would happen if you did? Wouldn't it just be like falling asleep? And why was I thinking about these things when there was a ghost standing next to my bed?

Even though I believed that people's souls go to Heaven, actually seeing the dead walking and talking in my bedroom caught me just a tad off guard. I wasn't sure if I could believe my eyes.

"Go ahead, believe your eyes," the ghost said, doing that freaky mind-meld thing again. "I am most definitely here. Thank goodness you can see and hear me." She looked around the room, smiling warmly. "Oh, my old room looks so wonderful! It's been so long."

I sat up in my bed and looked at her. Really looked at her. She wasn't shimmery or glowing blue or draped in a sheet. No rattling chains anywhere, she wore normal clothes: a blouse and some jeans, much like what she wore when I saw her that day at Foyles. She didn't even really look dead, to be honest. Fern Caldwell's ghost looked like a living, breathing Fern Caldwell, except sort of digitized. Like some kind of hologram, one that kept glitching like she had a weak signal.

"How can you be here? You're ..."

"Dead. Yes. An unfortunate and unanticipated turn of events, to say the least. I would have written faster if I'd known what he was up to, that bloody heathen. I hadn't even realized it was possible for him to do what he did. There are lots of other people like me who I've met since yesterday, all in the same predicament. Some in this very building. I'm no expert, mind you, but it seems that when there are things left to be done, the universe somehow finds a way to let you do them. Which brings me to why I'm here. I need your help."

"My help?" My heartbeat quickened to a gallop.

"Absolutely. Do you remember speaking to me at the book signing? You invited me to visit you."

"Yes, I did."

She raised an eyebrow and grinned. "I had a feeling you might be part of all this somehow. And given what's happened," Fern gestured to her ghostly self, "perhaps I was right."

I stared at her, completely dumbfounded. I didn't know which was more mind-blowing: seeing a ghost or hearing what she was telling me.

She put her hands on her hips and cocked her head. "You don't follow, do you? No, how could you? You need some backstory. Let's see, where to begin?" Her index finger tapped her pursed lips. "Your invitation, besides being quite polite, is quite possibly one of the reasons I'm able to appear to you. However, I think there is another."

"You are living in the room where I grew up. That seems to give us some kind of energy connection—again, this is a work in progress, but I'm relatively sure the theory is sound. And," she grinned, "I'd be willing to bet you have the gift. Second sight? I tried appearing to some friends back in Glastonbury and it didn't work at all. So, do you have second sight?"

"What … do you mean?" My heart nearly stopped beating.

"Have you ever known something was going to happen, before it did?"

I could barely breath. "You're talking about seeing dreams," I whispered.

When I was a little kid, I thought everyone's dreams sometimes became reality. You dreamed that you would see some baby ducks at the park and then the next day, there'd they be, waddling along. You dreamed your t-ball game would get rained out out, and it would. I was seven when I learned the truth.

One night I woke up covered with sweat, completely hysterical. I'd had a dream that my grandmother had died so, of course, I totally thought it was going to happen. It was the first really horrible thing I'd ever dreamt like this, and it freaked me out. I kept telling Mom, but she wouldn't believe it was true. Of course, she wouldn't. She didn't know I was getting this kind of thing right all the time. I didn't really talk about it. It was just part of my life. Besides, I was a seven-year-old kid.

But when we got the call from Grandma's assisted living place the next morning, saying Grandma had passed away in her sleep the night before, Mom was the one freaking out.

That was the day I learned I was different and not exactly in a good way—it was obvious by the look on my mom's face as the phone slid out of her hand and clattered to the floor. She stared at me like I was a creature from another planet. Thank God Claire had already left for school. She'd think I was even more of a freak than she already did.

As I got older, I realized that these dreams weren't just dreams. They were messages. Warnings, even. Okay, maybe I couldn't have saved my grandmother—she was 84 and it was probably her time—but if Mom had believed me, maybe I could've told Grandma that I loved her one more time. Because I did love her. She was a totally cool grandma, and I didn't tell her that near enough. But hey, I was seven.

Mom never told Claire or Dad, and we never talked about it after Grandma died. I only ever told one person about my dreams. Not Libby, that was for sure. Libby was the worst at keeping her mouth shut. If she got wind of something the rest of the school knew about it by lunch. She just couldn't keep a secret. It would sort of seep out of her, like she had holes in her secret-keeper or something.

The only person I'd told about my dreams was Colin. I'd never had a friend like him before, and I totally trusted him not to make fun of me or blab my secrets all over school. One time, Colin told me he liked country music. I guess he thought me being from Texas that I was into it, because he was surprised to find I hated it. We were still newish friends at the time, so I hated that he felt weird about it. So, to make things even, I told him something weird about myself. It actually felt great to talk to someone about the dreams and, luckily, he thought it was kinda cool. I wasn't sure if he actually believed me or was just a nice guy.

What would Colin think when he heard that Fern Caldwell's ghost had appeared in my bedroom? I wasn't sure what I thought about it.

Her ghost did that strange glitching thing again. I wondered what that felt like, or if she even felt it at all? She paced beside my bed. Actually, since her feet didn't quite reach the floor, it was more like gliding back and forth, with none of that up-and-down movement that happens with walking.

Fern pivoted and headed straight for the "shrine." I clutched the comforter to my chest as my face grew hot. Oh no. She was going to think I was a complete, stalker-level goon. But she smiled as she examined the display. "Tell me, Henderson Green. How many times have you read my books?"

I slid out of bed, ignoring the frigid wood beneath my feet. I was so relieved she wasn't horrified about the shrine, I almost forgot I was talking to a ghost. "Twenty? At least. Except for Sword Hunters ... " Suddenly, it felt like I'd swallowed a golf ball. "I haven't finished it yet. I meant to last night." The lump in my throat swelled up to tennis ball size. Oh cripes, I was going to cry. I was going to cry in front of Fern Caldwell.

She cocked her head to the side, studying me. The expression on her face was so kind, it made the tears come all the faster. "Ah, sweetheart. It's all right."

I swallowed hard, wiping the tears away with the back of my hand. "I just get so sad when I think there won't be any more books. I'm sorry, I know that seems selfish, seeing as how you're ... well, you know."

Fern turned back to the shelf of books. She reached out as if she was going to touch the cheek of King Arthur's illustrated face on the cover of Doorway to Avalon—the copy she'd signed that day at Foyles. "No, it's not selfish, not at all. It would be a great tragedy if the story could not continue. More than you even realize."

I shivered; one of those icy, uncontrollable tremors like you sometimes get after a sneeze. "What do you mean if the story could not continue? How could it?"

Fern Caldwell glanced back at me, her eyes brightening, her smile wide. "Well, that brings us back around to the reason I'm here, right? As I said, I need your help."

I took a step backward. "You did say that, yes, but I don't understand. How could I ever help you?"

Fern Caldwell floated past me and "sat" on my bed, pulling her legs up crisscross applesauce, as we used to say in preschool, so that she hovered a few inches above the covers. She rested her chin on her hand as if thinking about how to answer my question. She looked so young that I could easily imagine her as the little girl who grew up in this room. "You know, I wrote my first story right there," she said, indicating a spot to my right. "My desk was where that window seat is now. Father built the seat after I left for University." Her smile widened as she floated up and over to where the desk would have been years ago, gracefully unfolding her legs to sit on an invisible chair. A ghostly desk materialized in front of her, small and white with one single front drawer. The back of the desk dissolved into the window seat.

"Whoa," I breathed.

Fern Caldwell turned to me and grinned. "Fancy that! I just wished for my desk, and here it is. What fun."

Another shiver rattled me, the rain's chill seeping through the walls of the building and into my bones. I grabbed a blanket off the bed and wrapped myself in its warmth. "Is that really your old desk?" I whispered.

"Amazingly so," Fern Caldwell answered, voice alight in wonder. She picked up a ghostly sheet of paper. I could see the handwriting on it, a childish scribbling. "And this is my first story. Only a page of words, but I was so proud. Even then I was writing about Arthur. My grandmother told me the story for years, just the basic one most everyone knows—Merlin stealing the baby Arthur who grew up not knowing who he was until he pulled the sword from the stone. But I loved it. There was something so fascinating about it. When I grew older, I read everything I could get my hands on about King Arthur, Camelot … Avalon. I soon discovered all the different legends, and how nobody really knew which, if any, was the truth." She paused, looking at me. "I sat at this very desk the day I realized the secret."

"Secret?" I asked, my heart thumping wildly again.

Fern let the sheet of paper fall from her hand. Instead of fluttering to the floor, it broke up into a million tiny points of light and evaporated.

"Arthur lives. He is alive and waiting to be saved."

I rubbed my forehead. "So, you mean, you got the idea for the Sydney Wakefield books?"

Fern raised one eyebrow. "In a way." The desk disappeared and she floated toward me. Up close, she looked even more like a hologram, projected from who knows where. "Henderson. It is up to you and me to make sure the story runs its course. So much is at stake! Without our help

Sydney will never return to Glastonbury and that alone would be a terrible tragedy, but if we don't finish the stories, Sydney will never be able to free King Arthur. And if that doesn't happen, and soon, there could be terrible consequences."

My heartbeat pounded in my ears, so loudly I thought it would burst from my chest and parade around the room. "Hold on, I don't understand. You're talking like it's not just a story," I said, searching her face. "But, it is, right? Just a story?"

Fern smiled. "I think you already know the answer to that question."

Then, as if my brain was zapped by magic, I did know.

The stories ... were real.

Fern Caldwell's smile widened. "Yes," she whispered. "They are real. And with your help, I can complete my quest to save Sydney and rescue Arthur. The last book will be finished, it will be read, and it will be so." She nodded as if she hadn't said something completely mental. "We will have foiled Morgan le Fay, once and for all, and I will have my revenge on Modred."

My head spun. "Revenge? For what?"

Her expression frosted as she turned toward the window. Rain streaming down the glass. I could see it through her. The edge of her voice sharpened. "Why for killing me, of course."

Chapter 4

Modred, son of Morgan le Fay, nephew of King Arthur, had killed Fern Caldwell? "But, I don't understand. The BBC said you had a heart attack," I blurted, dumbfounded.

"Yes, well, the BBC isn't always accurate."

How could Modred be more than just a character in a story? "How is this possible?"

Fern turned away from the window, her smile sad. "I don't know how to answer that, dear boy. I wish I could." She raised her eyebrows. "The stories played about in my imagination for years while I was growing up. I wrote them down a million different times in a million different ways. But putting them down on paper isn't what brought them to life. It was after they were finally published that Sydney became part of the story. I've always believed that the magic comes from the reading. My fans have such overwhelming love for the characters. Powerful emotion like that has a magic all its own."

I stared at her. "But, how did you figure out everything was really happening in Avalon?"

Her expression darkened. "I began to suspect when Sydney disappeared."

"Sydney. You mean your neighbor in Glastonbury?" I paused, my brain processing. "Are you saying she is the real Sydney Wakefield?"

Fern turned to the window again, the tone of her voice distant. "Her name is Sydney Temple. She and I became very close while I was writing the first book, so I named the character for her. When she first disappeared, I thought someone had taken her. But once the dreams began, I knew she was lost."

I perched on the edge of the bed, pulling the blanket tighter around me as I listened.

"The idea of Morgan trapping Arthur in Avalon when she sailed away with him after the battle of Camlann had kicked about in my mind since I was a young girl. After I moved to Glastonbury to work on the story, I thought, what if someone found a way into Avalon to rescue Arthur from Morgan's curse?

"I'd always believed that Glastonbury was Avalon. My parents took me for a visit when I was about your age and the moment I arrived in Glastonbury I felt something click into place, deep in my soul. The air smelled better, the sky seemed bluer. Everything just seemed 'right' in Glastonbury.

"As soon as I graduated University, I moved there. And Sydney became like a little sister to me," Fern went on, wistfully. "She showed me the sites, led me on my first walk up the Tor, and showed me the Living Rock. That night, I had a dream. No, more than a dream. It was so vivid, so real. Unlike any dream I'd ever had before. It felt more like a memory. Does that make sense?"

I nodded, unable to speak.

"I dreamed that Sydney touched The Living Rock and opened a doorway. I saw the light, I felt Arthur inside, calling to me. I knew, this was the way in to Avalon."

"Wicked," I breathed, as mesmerized by her spoken words as much as I ever was by her books.

"When I woke, I felt compelled to write it. Of course, if I'd known," Fern trailed off, then turned back to me. "But that's not the issue for now. The issue is that I need your help. The final book cannot be left unfinished. We must find a way to get it written, so we can bring Sydney home." She floated closer, and gave me a determined look. "I can't do it without help, Henderson. Will you help me?"

"Wait, what?" I put my hands to my head. Talk about dreaming, that had to be what was happening to me. I had to be dreaming, right? There was no way Fern Caldwell's ghost was asking me to help her finish the last book of her Sydney Wakefield series, in order to rescue the real Sydney, and King Arthur, from Morgan le Fay's dark Avalon. It was too fantastical. "But," I stammered, questions spinning in my mind. "I still don't understand how you know Sydney is in Avalon?"

Fern took on a glow and her smile softened. "Every night after that first night, I had those vivid dreams. They happened like a story. Each chapter playing out as I slept. And every night, I'd wake and write it down. That dream journal became Doorway to Avalon. I hardly even edited the thing." She paused, choosing her words carefully. "It was like I was channeling the story, like someone else was writing it through me. Nothing like this had ever happened to me before.

"When I reached Doorway's last chapter, I had this intense need to get it published. I mean, that was always my goal, to make a living as an author, but this need was different. I pushed the story on everyone I could, feeling this need to have it read. Stanley was the first agent I approached, and he signed me immediately. The first publisher who read it, bought it. Everything just fell into place, like it was meant to happen.

"After Sydney disappeared, when we were deep in the search for her, I confessed to Sydney's grandfather about the dreams. I'd almost finished the second book by that time. Franklin and I had been close before, but during the search for Sydney we leaned on each other quite heavily. So, it was natural that I was the one he would tell about his own dreams. They started when Sydney disappeared." Her voice trembled and I saw a twinkle of tears in her eyes. "We were having the same dreams. The exact same dreams. At the same time."

Fern crossed her arms across her middle, like she needed to give herself a hug. "Then, about a week after Sydney disappeared, Arthur appeared in one of my dreams. This dream was different. In all my other dreams, Arthur was trapped in the glass coffin, inside the Avalon castle. He wasn't a participant; Sydney was trying to rescue him. But here he was, standing beside my bed, telling me Sydney needed my help. He said I wasn't supposed to just write what I saw in my dreams. I needed to write what should happen.

"As soon as I woke up, I did just that. I changed the story, just a little. And do you know what? That night, I dreamed what I'd written."

"Whoa," I breathed, completely immersed in her words.

"The following morning, Franklin said his had changed as well!" Her eyes sparkled, knowingly. "It sounds completely crazy, I know."

I was talking to a ghost. We were long past crazy. "So, you could control the story. Then why didn't you just have Sydney free Arthur and bring her home?" I asked. "Why keep it going for another book?"

She smiled, like she knew I was going to ask that. "I tried. I wrote faster than I'd ever done. I sent it off to my publisher, and they thought I'd lost my mind. Asked if I'd actually written it or not. You see, when I made it too easy for Sydney and Arthur to escape and, the story kind of fell apart. It wasn't any fun to read anymore. Thank goodness, the first book was selling so well, or I think the publisher would have dropped me. Stanley, too." She smiled. "I realized it wasn't just writing the story that would save Arthur and Sydney, but writing a story the reader would love. That love was an essential part of the magic. My writing was just the conduit."

I blinked. "Conduit?"

"The connection. Remember, it wasn't until that first book became popular and was read by so many that Sydney disappeared. It didn't happen when I typed the story on the page, or even when the pages were printed out. The power was in the reader's hands. It had to be told properly, in a way a reader would love."

"But how do you know how to do that?" I breathed.

Fern shrugged. "I don't know, I just feel it. It's part of the magic, I suppose. Think of how you feel when you read my books. Do you believe it?"

"Oh, yes. Absolutely." When I was deep in the pages of a Sydney Wakefield book, it felt like it was real. "Yeah," I breathed. "I totally believe."

Fern smiled. "The real magic of a beloved story goes far beyond putting words on paper. And I was so close to finishing Into the Faraway."

"Is that the title? We've been waiting for months to hear about—" I froze. "Hey! What's happening? I think you're fading!"

Fern looked down at herself. "Blast! I'm out of time."

"But wait, you can't go yet! You haven't told me about Modred! How did he come through to our world to get to you?"

"Later, Henderson, I promise. Right now, you must listen!" Fern held up a hand as I began to protest. "Go to Glastonbury, as soon as you can find a way."

My mouth fell open. "Glastonbury!" I sputtered. "But—"

"I know it will be difficult, but you must. Go to The Chalice Bookshop, near the Market Square at the intersection of High Street and Magdalene. Talk to Franklin Temple. He runs the bookstore. He has an extra key to my flat. Look in—" Then I couldn't hear her anymore, and I could barely see her. My heart ached.

"No, please don't go!" Fern's lips kept moving but I couldn't hear what she said. She clasped her hands together, begging me. Then, she was gone.

My room had never seemed so dark and quiet, the only sound the rain against the window.

Holy macaroni.

Nobody was going to believe this. Nobody! I wasn't even sure if I actually believed it. Was she just a dream? Or did a real ghost just show up in my bedroom?

I burrowed deep under my covers to stop myself from shaking, pulling my lucky rock out from under my pillow. With it in my hand, I lay there listening to the patter of the rain, wondering what in the world I was going to do now.

There it was: the long, jeweled box Sydney and Isabelle had found beneath Morgan le Fay's bed. If only they'd known before that it held Excalibur's Scabbard, Sydney and Melora wouldn't have to sneak back into the castle to steal it from under Morgan's nose.

Sydney kept watch in the darkened hallway, hoping the steaming hot draught Melora had concocted, and delivered to her under the guise of one of Morgan's many servants, would knock Morgan out soon, so that they could escape with the treasure.

The bedchamber door creaked and Melora's face appeared. "Come along then," she grinned. "The evil queen shall not give us trouble."

SYDNEY WAKEFIELD
AND THE SECRET OF THE TOR

CHAPTER 5

I remember the day I saw the first Sydney Wakefield movie so clearly. Colin, Libby and I were completely chuffed, as they say over here. We'd been counting down the days ever since Mom snagged us tickets to a special VIP screening the day after the London premiere. Okay, sometimes Mom's job was pretty cool.

With large buckets of double-butter, extra salt popcorn in our laps and sodas with no ice in the cup holders of our theater chairs, we sat back as the story that had previously lived only in my imagination came to brilliant life. Excitement buzzed through my veins from the opening scene where this amazing drone footage made us feel like we swooped down from the clouds over Glastonbury, moving quickly toward a huge, grassy hill called the Tor. We flew up its slope toward the ancient ruins of St. Michael's, the tower that perched on top like a stone guard looming over the town. Then the scene changed and we were flying over cute little houses and shops like the one Sydney's grandfather ran.

I glanced at my friends, seeing the same blissful grin on their faces that I knew had to be on mine. When I turned my eyes back to the screen, the drone shot had changed to a close-up of an older man with a long, grey ponytail: this was obviously Sydney's grandfather, Franklin Wakefield. He was a King Arthur historian who ran bookshop that only sold books about King Arthur. He lived in Glastonbury since it was such a hot spot for King Arthur legends. And at this moment in the movie, he was telling Sydney about one of them.

"The Living Rock, again?" he asked with a chuckle as he tucked a wooden pipe into the crook of his mouth. "Why do you always want to hear this story, Sydney? You know it so well, you could tell it to me!"

"It's my favorite," Tara Benjamin said, acting the part of Sydney Wakefield. She walked across the flat and flopped onto an old couch. "And you tell it so much better. Please, Grandfather?"

Franklin Wakefield rocked in an easy chair next to a big stone hearth. "As you wish, my dear." He closed his eyes and began. As he spoke, the shot returned to the Tor, moving over its green lawns toward the place in question.

"Near the base of the Tor stands a magical stone that some, who believe in this sort of thing, call the Living Rock. Many years ago, the rock was a tall, ancient marker. But the years have worn it down and now all that is left are two large boulders. According to legend, this is the doorway into Avalon: the magical island where Morgan le Fay took King Arthur to be healed from the wounds he sustained at the hand of his nephew, Modred, in that final battle at Camlann."

Back to Franklin, who took a long pull on the pipe and blew a stream of snow white smoke into the air. "There are some who feel strange vibrations when they touch the Living Rock at the moment of sunrise or sunset. But is it actually a doorway into Avalon? If so, it has not opened for anyone who lives to tell about it."

You could tell by Sydney's expression that she totally dug this story; and that she'd been thinking about trying it out for a long time.

In the next scene, it was late afternoon as Sydney delivered a package for her grandfather. On the way home, she rode her bike past a path entrance to a woody area. A sign read "Glastonbury Tor." Sydney looked at the setting sun, as it neared the horizon, considering. Next thing you know, Sydney was pushing her bike up the Tor's path. As she reached the Rock and dropped her bike on the grass, she stretched out a shaking hand just as the last glimpse of the sun dipped under the horizon behind her.

Her hand settled on the stone. At first nothing happened. But then the ground started to tremble and swirls of mist blew in around her. Then it opened up right before her—the Doorway to Avalon—like a huge split in the picture of reality, creating a yawning hole right in the side of the Tor.

The music swelled dramatically as Sydney tentatively approached the Doorway. Suddenly, she was yanked forward. Sydney resisted, but the force was too powerful. It pulled her toward the Doorway, sucking the mist along for the ride. Then she was gone, with only a few tendrils of mist left behind to dissipate into the twilight.

Colin, Libby, and I cheered along with the rest of the audience. Sydney had found Avalon. Her adventure had begun.

The morning after the ghost of Fern Caldwell showed up at the foot of my bed, I did a pretty good job of convincing myself the whole thing hadn't happened. At all. Just a dream.

Hey, stress can do terrible things to a person, and I knew I was really upset over Fern's death, so it would be very natural to dream that her ghost visited me.

I told myself this over and over as I microwaved some instant oatmeal and slugged down a glass of orange juice before leaving for school. "Just a dream," I mumbled as I jammed my shirttails into my pants and slipped on my jacket. Just a wacky, out-there dream.

Although Mom still was being nice about the whole bump on the head thing, she wasn't about to let me stay home. I was nervous about going back, figuring everyone knew about the scene I'd made the day before. I could only imagine the crap I was going to get—look, there goes Henderson Green, world-famous fainter.

Surprisingly, nobody called me that, but they had some other names for me: Crybaby was a nice one. A couple of ninth-year boys bumped into me on purpose on the way to Lit class. "Oh, so sorry, mate!" one of them said, his sarcasm about as subtle as a shaved head. "Uh oh, you gonna cry?" Their laughter followed me into Mrs. Baines' classroom. I tried to ignore them or, at least, tried to act like I didn't care. I failed on both.

Mrs. Baines taught sixth-, seventh-, and eighth-year Literature, and even though I loved to read more than anything in the world, I couldn't stand her class. She had a nasty way of making me feel about two feet tall. I don't think she liked Americans much and she hated the Sydney Wakefield books. She didn't consider them 'literature,' a word that in her appropriately stuffy British accent sounded even snobbier. Pop pulp was a term she'd thrown around about the books more than once, as if anything that appealed to more than a handful of people wasn't worthy of the ink used to print it.

At the end of last year, Mrs. Baines had actually given us an exiting assignment: we were to write our own chapter from a favorite work of— wait for it—literature, in the style of the author who originally created it. Be creative, Mrs. Baines encouraged. I don't think she even realized she was giving us a fan fic assignment. I don't think she knew fan fic was even a thing. But none of us told her. Ideas immediately flooded my head and I was scribbling down ideas before Baines even finished handing out the rubrics.

I knew Baines hated Fern Caldwell, but I'd decided to choose my favorite author anyway. I wrote the first chapter of Sydney Wakefield and The Sword Hunters, which at the time was the third book about to be released for the summer holiday. My first chapter started where Fern left off at the end of her second book: Sydney and Sir Bedivere arriving at the Tor in Avalon to find Excalibur. They knew Morgan had it hidden somewhere in the tunnels beneath the Tor. They also knew Sydney could cross Morgan le Fay's white circles. Morgan put these magically protective barriers around a ton of stuff, and for most people their magic created an invisible wall. But they didn't work on Sydney. Bedivere figured Morgan had relied on those magic circles to protect the Sword, not knowing Sydney could just walk over and pick it up.

The two travelled with Isabelle, Gavin, and their mother, Melora— Merlin's friends who helped Sydney and Sir Bedivere steal Excalibur's jeweled Scabbard from Morgan le Fay's bedchambers. Because the Scabbard was one of the three elements needed to break the curse over Arthur, it was kept apart from its sword, Excalibur—also one of the elements. The third was still a mystery.

In my chapter, I speculated about the third element. By the way, I was right. When the book came out a few weeks later, I humble bragged about that for a while until Colin told me it was annoying. Yes, the fan base had figured it out too, but I kept up with the Sydney Wakefield Reddit threads, so I knew I was one of the first. In the actual book, the group encountered a secret colony of elves who tells them how to find the third element: The Holy Grail.

Of course.

My chapter definitely wasn't Fern Caldwell caliber, but it was okay. Even Mrs. Baines gave it a passing grade. Barely, though. She sure didn't think I had a future as a writer.

I should have told that to Fern Caldwell's ghost last night.

Except there was no ghost. She wasn't real. That was just a dream!

I refused to believe it, even when my brain kept trying to convince me it was true. Seriously, it had to be a dream because, if it wasn't, that meant I had to figure out how to get to Glastonbury on my own. And that was just impossible.

Not thrilled to have Baines for my Lit teacher again this year, missing her class was about the only good thing that happened yesterday. Finding an empty seat, I tried to shake off visions of the night before. Mrs. Baines did not seem at all upset that the literary world had lost a great contributor. She didn't even mention Fern Caldwell's shocking death, which really ticked me off. She did have something to say about me, though.

"Master Green! Glad to have you with us this morning," Baines crowed in her pinched voice. "We missed you yesterday."

I stared at her, trying to keep my emotions off my face. I wouldn't serve me well to let her see how much I hated her.

"Now class," she went on, "I have a few questions for you to answer regarding last night's reading assignment, so books away please."

The entire class groaned, me included. With a cold smile, Baines placed the pop quiz on my desk and moved on down the row. Really? On the second day of school? That she gave homework the first night wasn't surprising, but a pop quiz so soon was cruel, even for her.

The rest of my day progressed about as well. I dropped my tray during lunch, splashing milk all over Hugh Frank, the biggest bully in eighth year. (I was lucky the headmaster was right there too or no doubt Hugh would have pounded me into oblivion.) Then I tripped over my trainers in P.E. and banged my elbow so hard it bruised. And I never could get my new locker combination to work, so I ended up late to everything, and carrying my books around with me.

Worse than all that, I couldn't stop thinking about Fern Caldwell. I decided not to mention the weird dream to Colin. I did NOT see dead people, especially ghosts of newly dead authors. This was NOT one of my seeing dreams.

Colin and I walked home together. It was about a half hour walk, or a five-minute tube ride, but it was a nice day so we walked. He was going on and on about some girl in his Maths class, but I wasn't really paying attention. I just nodded at the right moments, and he kept on going. When we reached my street, he walked with me to our flat as usual. His house was a few blocks farther, and even though it was a little out of his way to detour down my street first, he always did.

I was so shocked to see Fern Caldwell sitting on my front stoop that I nearly jumped out of my skin. What's more, Colin clearly did not see her. He just kept on walking, asking if I wanted to ride bikes to school tomorrow.

"Ummmm, sure?" I stammered, standing there on the sidewalk, completely mystified. Did he not see her? I looked at Colin, then at Fern, then back at Colin. "Hey, uh, do you see anything strange around here?"

Colin scanned up and down the street, giving me a curious look. "No. Everything looks just like it always does. You okay, mate? You've been odd all day."

I shook my head. "You seriously don't see anyone sitting on my front steps?"

He scowled. "Are you zonked? That bump on your head knock your brain loose or what?"

I rubbed the sore spot. "No, I'm fine. But … you really don't see anyone?" I looked right at Fern and she waggled her fingers at me.

"Get some rest, chum. I'll swing by in the morning, 'kay? Cheers." And with that, he left me there.

With the ghost.

"I'm really here."

I glanced at Colin who had reached the end of the street already. "No, you can't be," I stage-whispered at her. "You're just my grieving imagination, conjuring up something to make me feel better about a terrible loss I'm suffering. Please, go away!" I rushed past her to shove my key into the lock. Inside, I slammed it shut and leaned against it.

I needed a Coke.

After grabbing a can from the fridge, I made my way upstairs to my room—where I found Fern floating beside my Sydney Wakefield shrine in the corner.

"Henderson, I know this is a tough thing to swallow, but I'm not going away until you believe in me." She folded her arms across her chest. "Sorry I disappeared on you last night. I don't have a lot of control over this."

Was I truly going crazy? The idea that it was real made my heart pound in sort of a wonderful way. "Look, I want to believe. It would be so great if it were true. But it doesn't matter, because even if I did believe that this is real, I still can't help you. I'm thirteen! How do I get out to some little country town hundreds of miles away?"

"I may have an idea." Fern grinned, nodding toward the books. "Read the acknowledgement page in Doorway."

With a sigh, I pulled my copy of Doorway to Avalon off the shelf and flipped through the first pages. I read it aloud. "Many thanks to Stanley Doonesbury for his diligence, steadfast encouragement, and tireless hounding of many editors. If it weren't for you, this book would not exist."

Stanley Doonesbury. Fern's literary agent. The same guy I had seen on TV the night before. I certainly needed a grown up's help if I was going to get to Glastonbury … But only if that was something I was going to do, and it most certainly was not, since none of this was real. I turned to Fern to tell her just that, but she was gone again. Guess she still needed some work on sticking around. I tossed the book on my desk and sunk into the chair, staring at my iMac, a birthday present from my dad last year.

I stared at the blank screen. Then, with a sigh, I brought my computer out of sleep mode. Then I Googled Stanley Doonesbury.

He was a senior agent with Callahan and Willemshire in London. Their offices were over by Hyde Park, not far from our flat. Okay, so what was I doing, Googling this guy? Was I truly considering this?

Let's just say I was, I told myself. The only way to get to Glastonbury was with some adult assistance. But how could I convince this guy about Fern when I wasn't even sure I believed it myself?

I imagined how cool it would be to see the place where Fern Caldwell lived and wrote, to track down an original unfinished manuscript from one of the most famous sets of books on the planet— the idea was so amazing, I wanted it to be true. How mind-blowing to be the one to help Fern Caldwell write the last Sydney Wakefield book, not to mention save Sydney and King Arthur!

Maybe I would just go visit Mr. Stanley Doonesbury and see what he said when I told him about Fern. Maybe he wouldn't be shocked or surprised at all, and he'd immediately drive me to Glastonbury to fetch the manuscript. Maybe he'd be the kind of grown up who actually believed in magic, and wouldn't doubt the mental story of some thirteen-year-old kid he just met.

Or, maybe not.

The tunnels snaked through the heart of the Tor, twisting and turning. It was like some sort of cursed maze from which they would never escape. The others followed Sydney blindly believing she knew something they didn't, sure she would lead them to their prize: one of the keys to breaking the curse. They all trusted her to choose direction when the paths forked, and panic was beginning to take an icy hold on her heart as the tunnels continued to lead nowhere. Then, without warning, the passageway opened into an enormous cavern.

The yawning space was lit with hundreds of thick, stumpy candles floating in midair, dripping wax. They flickered a warning, illuminating a thick, white chalk circle on the dirty cavern floor. Hovering magically in the middle of it was the most beautiful thing Sydney had ever seen.

The Sword. Excalibur.

SYDNEY WAKEFIELD
AND THE SECRET OF THE TOR

CHAPTER 6

My sister Claire loved to torture me. She did it whenever she had the chance which, unfortunately, was often. And her favorite thing to torture me about was Sydney Wakefield.

"What a dumb story, I can't believe you're so into it." On the evening before the first day of school, Claire railed on me because I couldn't stop talking about my plans to finish the book that night. We were working a thousand-piece puzzle of Big Ben, and not very well. Puzzle making was one of my mom's brilliant schemes to get Claire and me to "bond." She was tired of us arguing all the time and loved seeing us working together. Of course, the puzzle just gave us something else to argue about.

"You better watch what you say," I blasted back at my sister. Claire gave me an over-done, fake tremble to show how little my fury terrified her. "What do you know about it anyway?" I snarled. "Everyone's read it but you."

Claire huffed. "Exactly! Educated people read things out of the mainstream." This was the kind of thing Claire said all the time. She loved to use the word "educated," as if I was anything but.

"Whatever." I spotted a puzzle piece with a section of Big Ben's face and grabbed it before Claire could. "You can't talk trash about books you haven't read. Mom says you can't dislike something if you haven't tried it."

"She just told you that to get you to eat broccoli," Claire sneered, totally ignoring the puzzle now, which was fine by me. I'd rather work the thing myself anyway. "Sydney Wakefield is just a pop culture Phenom and you're just one of the sheep on the bandwagon."

I tried not to let her get to me, really, I did. I thought what Mom's words—I could stop the arguments before they started if I didn't react. Easy for her to say. She wasn't the one getting verbally abused every time she turned around.

But the sheep comment? I couldn't just let that slide. It wasn't just the popularity of the Sydney Wakefield books that made me want to read them. I've always been into stories about medieval times, knights, dragons, and castles. And I've read tons of other King Arthur stories. I just happened to like the Sydney Wakefield ones best.

Maybe that was because those books took a bunch of different stuff from all the old King Arthur legends for a whole new story. For instance, according to the original legend, Arthur was terribly wounded in battle by his nephew Modred. Knowing he was going to die, Arthur told Sir Bedivere to throw his sword, Excalibur, into the lake, since he'd promised to return it to the mysterious Lady of the Lake who'd given it to him. Then, Morgan le Fay sailed Arthur away to the Isle of Avalon, vowing to heal Arthur and protect him until it was time for him to return and rule "all of the Britons"—what they called the UK a long time ago. As the once and future King, Arthur was supposed to return someday … and lots of people actually believed it to be true.

But in the Sydney Wakefield books, Morgan le Fay stood in for the Lady of the Lake when Sir Bedivere threw Excalibur back. Morgan had previously stolen Excalibur's magical Scabbard from Arthur, something that protected him from being wounded. That theft allowed her to set up the chance for Arthur to actually lose that final battle against Modred, her son. She wanted him to be king, and she knew once she had both the Scabbard and Excalibur, she would have enough power to create the kingdom where he could rule. Dark Avalon.

Arthur didn't die in that battle, though. He just almost died. And Morgan took his nearly dead body to Dark Avalon and displayed it in a glass coffin in the middle of the castle courtyard, to remind all the shadow people who were also trapped in Dark Avalon that Morgan le Fay was the one in control.

In the original legends, Arthur's father fell in love with Morgan's mother, and killed her father to marry her. Morgan always pretended to be Arthur's faithful and true sister, but it was a big, fat lie. She hated him. And she raised her son Modred to hate him just as much. So, in the

Sydney Wakefield books, it became her final revenge to keep Arthur barely alive and helpless, forced to watch her son rule.

The shadow people of Dark Avalon included a few of the Round Table Knights, like Sir Bedivere, but not Lancelot who had run away to France after Arthur found out he was in love with Queen Guinevere. She wasn't in Avalon either, as she had left Camelot in shame, and ended up becoming a nun.

At least, that was the theory. Sydney Wakefield fan sites, blogs, and Reddit threads listed hundreds of other theories, but the reason for Guinevere or Lancelot's absence from the stories hadn't yet been explained as of book three. I'd read somewhere that Fern Caldwell refused to answer questions about why these two famous characters weren't a part of her stories.

I made a mental not to ask her myself. She owed me, right?

The shadow Knights in Morgan's Dark Avalon were kept locked up in the dungeons so they wouldn't cause trouble. Morgan and Modred were the only two non-shadow, living people in Avalon. And the Scabbard's magic made them immortal.

"Okay, freak-a-zoid," Claire snipped, grabbing a puzzle piece but not doing anything with it. "Here's a question … if Sydney Wakefield is all about King Arthur, why no Lancelot, Guinevere or Merlin in the stories?"

"Well, I don't know about the first two, nobody's figured that out yet, but I'll tell you about Merlin," I answered, lifting an eyebrow. "Morgan le Fay designed her Dark Avalon to keep him out. See, she used to be Merlin's student and she knew if there was anyone who could mess up her plans it would be him. Everyone, including Merlin, had to believe Arthur had sailed off to Avalon to be healed. She planted that story and made sure it became legend. So now, that's what everybody thinks is the real story."

"Hold on," Claire held up the puzzle piece. "Merlin had to know the legend was false. What about the prophecy? Doesn't Bedivere tell Sydney she's the one from Merlin's Prophecy?"

My eyes narrowed. "I thought you didn't read the books?"

Claire dropped the puzzle piece and shook her arm so the bangles of bracelets around her wrist jangled. "Don't be so suspicious and dramatic. I saw the first movie at someone's house one night, big deal."

"You did?"

"Completely infantile." Her snark was razor sharp.

I sighed, not sure what to think about this revelation, but decided not to press it with Mom in the next room. I could 100% guarantee that she was listening in. "Well, the shadow people in Dark Avalon do believe Merlin dreamt the Prophecy about Sydney being destined to save Arthur from the glass coffin. But we don't know if that's true or not."

Talking about the Sydney Wakefield books always got me hyped, and I'd always wished it was something Claire and I could share. It'd be so great if she was a fan too, then we might actually have something to talk about without fighting. My words spilled out quickly. "They'd heard about the Prophecy, about Sydney Wakefield, for as long as they could remember. But for them, time doesn't exist. They're trapped in this limbo, never growing old, nothing changing, day after day. For years! Then, Sydney shows up and they think she is the one to break the curse."

Claire starts to say something, but I plunge forward, cutting her off. "Morgan knows this too, which is why she has Sydney thrown into the dungeon. Sydney scares her. Morgan can't figure out how she made it through the magical doorway because it was only supposed to work for her and Modred. In the dungeons, Sydney meets Sir Bedivere and he tells her all about the Prophecy and of course Sydney freaks out, I mean, who wouldn't? Can you imagine finding out you're the one who is suppose to rescue an entire realm of souls? And King Arthur? The pressure! And then—"

"HG, stop! I don't need a complete book report!" Claire looked at me, more amused than annoyed for once. "Look, I know you want me to read these books, but it's not gonna happen, so just drop it! I've got more important literary works to read."

There she went with the literary thing again. I was beginning to hate that word. Claire was the only person I'd ever known who liked reading the books assigned in school. Personally, I didn't understand why Fern Caldwell's books weren't on our reading lists.

Claire decided to explain. "I prefer books that aren't so ... fantastical. Seriously, HG, fairy tales are so plebian. And it takes you all holiday to finish one simple story."

I tried to let it go. Really, I did.

"They aren't fairy tales, you book snob! Just because something has a little magic in it, doesn't make it—"

"Stop arguing!" Mom warned from the kitchen, her words wafting into the room along with the spicy smell of taco meat. Thank goodness it was almost dinnertime, I thought. Because that meant bedtime was just around the corner and once Mom and Claire were asleep, the issue of my finishing the book would be a thing of the past.

Claire scowled at me, angry that my volume had gotten her into trouble. "Okay, Mom." Then she smiled wickedly and her words became sticky sweet. "I'm sorry, it's all my fault." She grinned, got up from the game table and skipped past my half-hearted attempt at a kick in her direction. "Do you need any help in the kitchen? Your kind, obedient daughter is ready to help!"

I heard Mom snort at that, so at least she wasn't buying Claire's act. I heaved a sigh and turned back to the puzzle, but my mind wasn't on it. Claire had gotten me thinking about Sydney Wakefield, and now all I wanted to do was sneak up to my room and read that last chapter of Sword Hunters. But I couldn't cheat. I had to wait until midnight.

After tacos, we celebrated the last night of summer holiday with big bowls of ice cream topped with Oreo crumbles, my favorite dessert. Claire complained about gaining weight and how she wasn't going to fit into her uniform in the morning. I rolled my eyes so hard it actually gave me a headache.

After dinner I took a shower, brushed my teeth, and got in bed to wait for midnight. Which then came and went as I slept.

Now, Colin and I waited as the lift delivered us to the eighth floor, and Stanley Doonesbury's literary agency. We both rode silently, me lost in thought about a dream I'd had that morning. Yes, it was one of those dreams. Except this time, I wasn't dreaming about something that was about to happen, but something that already had. I felt sure of it.

In the dream, I flew over the town of Glastonbury, looking down on it, kind of like at the beginning of the Doorway to Avalon movie, except it was a dark night. I sensed some malicious force making its way down from the Glastonbury Tor. Then I saw him. His dark cape swirled around him as he strode through the quiet town, unafraid of being seen. I could tell he was evil just by how he moved.

And then, I could hear his thoughts. I realized he was about to commit the act that would save his kingdom, or so he believed. After tonight, he was sure his troubles would all be over and that wretched little girl and her cohorts would be history.

"HG? You okay?"

The doors to the lift had opened to an office lobby. A pretty woman sat at a desk. She and Colin both stared at me, waiting.

"Oh, right. Sorry." I stepped out into the sleekly decorated waiting area. Colin followed me. "We're here to see Stanley Doonesbury?" I said it like a question, turning it up at the end. I should have made it more like a statement, more confident. But sometimes I was wimpy like that. I cleared my throat, pushing back my shoulders and trying to stand taller than my five feet five inches.

"I'm sorry. Mr. Doonesbury is unavailable this afternoon."

Colin and I exchanged a glance. "But we really need to see him. It's about Fern Caldwell."

The perky receptionist gave us a sincerely sympathetic look. "I'm terribly sorry, young man. He wishes he could meet with every fan who is as heartbroken as he, but it's just impossible."

Colin cleared his throat and shifted uneasily. He didn't look at all happy that I'd talked him into accompanying me to Callahan and Willemshire. In fact, he looked incredibly pale and uncomfortable.

We'd ridden our bikes home from school together and I'd decided it was time to come clean about what was going on. We'd sat on the stoop—no ghost this time—and I'd told him everything. Despite his initial amazement, Colin seemed to believe me. But the closer we got to Doonesbury's office, the more hesitant he got.

"Please, miss," I begged, in my sweetest, most polite voice; the one I used on Mom when truly desperate. "It's really important that I talk to Mr. Doonesbury today. It's about the new Fern Caldwell book, Into the Faraway."

Confusion softened her kind expression, her brow bunching up. "Uh, wait right here a moment," she stammered, then hurried across the waiting area and through a tall dark wooden door.

As soon as it shut behind her Colin started in on me. "Blimey, HG, this is absolutely, 100% the most mental thing you've ever done. What was going on with you in the lift, back there? You were completely out of it."

"I need you to back me up on this," I begged, ignoring his question. "Even if you don't totally believe me. I know it sounds crazy. But I've got to get to Glastonbury, and Stanley Doonesbury is the perfect adult to make that happen."

Colin collapsed into a cushy, red velvet chair in the waiting area. "I wish you could hear yourself. You sound certifiable. First you tell me you were visited by Fern Caldwell's ghost, the same ghost you say was sitting on your front steps yesterday -- although I didn't see her. You say she told you that the Sydney Wakefield books are real, and that the fourth one must be finished so that King Arthur, who is also real, can be saved, just like in the books. Oh, and that there's a real Sydney Wakefield, and she's trapped there, too. Am I getting it so far?"

I glared at him, frustrated. "Seems like you understand everything perfectly, Colin." I crossed my arms across my chest. I knew it would be tough convincing Stanley Doonesbury, but Colin knew me well enough to know I wouldn't lie about a thing like this.

"Why you? Of all the Sydney Wakefield fans in the world, why are you the only one who can help Fern Caldwell? I mean, you're a Yank!"

I paused, ignoring the dig at my citizenship. "Fern has some theories. Maybe because of where I live. It gives us some sort of connection. Plus, I'm, well, you know ... "

"Yeah, yeah, psychic and all." Colin sighed, sounding exhausted. "I can't believe I'm letting myself believe you."

"Imagine how he's going to react," I said with a grin, jerking a thumb toward the closed door of Stanley Doonesbury's office.

Colin smiled thinly, then his eyes widened as the door opened. "There he is," Colin murmured.

I turned to face Stanley Doonesbury. He looked a lot shorter than he did on TV. He was a little troll-like man with longish brown hair that grew only around the back three-quarters of his head. It hung loose, about to his shoulders. Maybe he was going for a Lord of the Rings look—somewhere between a Hobbit and a Dwarf. On top, he was completely bald. If he'd worn brown robes, he would have looked more like a monk than someone from Middle Earth. He had an enormous nose that hooked at the end and a thick uni-brow, like a wiry caterpillar above his eyes. He wore dark, polished shoes that poked out from beneath the overly long pant legs of a dark gold suit. I'd never seen a gold suit before. He even wore a matching gold vest beneath his jacket, with a round watch snaking out of the pocket, which he studied before snapping shut.

"Now then, what's all this about, gents?" His voice was low and gravelly, his accent refined like he was royalty or something. I hesitated. He just didn't seem like the kind of person Fern Caldwell would entrust with such important stuff. He seemed like a fairy tale character pretending to be an average, ordinary guy. But I had no choice but to trust him.

"I need your help," I began, not comfortable explaining my plight right there in the lobby, especially with the receptionist standing right there. "Could we, uh, talk in your office?"

Doonesbury narrowed his eyes, but something had intrigued him enough to see us, so I decided to go for it.

"It's a matter of life and death. Fern Caldwell's death, to be exact."

Doonesbury's bushy eyebrow rose. "Hmm," he considered, studying me like an algebra book. "Lindsay, hold my calls for five minutes, please. After you, gentlemen."

He swept an arm toward his office, and I took the cue to step through the doorway ahead of him. Colin followed close behind. The room had quite the view. The eighth-floor windows overlooked Hyde Park and an enormous expanse of trees. Their intertwined branches created a sea of leafy green sprinkled autumn red and orange. Doonesbury sank into a tall-backed chair behind the massive dark-wood desk, leaning back and lacing his fingers over his belly as Colin and I sat in the leather armchairs.

"Here's the deal, Mr. Doonesbury. This is going to sound strange, maybe even a little bit … well, crazy." I paused, choosing my words carefully. "Fern Caldwell didn't finish book four before she died, and although you might think finishing it is no longer a possibility, I am here to tell you differently. It's super important the book gets finished. And published. And read by everyone who loves her books."

I looked at Colin, who'd turned green. I thought for a minute he might cut and run, but then he motioned for me to go on. I turned my eyes back to Doonesbury, who stared at me with a stunned expression.

"The thing is, Mr. Doonesbury, sir," I continued politely, as good manners certainly weren't going to hurt anything. "I live in the flat where

Fern Caldwell grew up, the one in Chelsea. I'm also, well ..." I looked at Colin for a suggestion. His eyes swiveled back to Doonesbury.

"Psychic?" Colin offered, his voice squeaky.

"Yes, psychic." Doonesbury was going to have us hauled away; one more second and he'd be calling building security.

He finally spoke. "You're psychic." His tone sounded like he was fighting back laughter.

"Actually, yes. See, I have these dreams sometimes and they, kind of ... come true. She said I have second sight. I guess that's why I can see her, even though nobody else seems to be able to."

"Who?" Doonesbury chewed thoughtfully on the end of an expensive-looking pen, his expression amused.

"Fern Caldwell," I said, looking back and forth between him and Colin.

One corner of Doonesbury's mouth turned up slightly. "Fern Caldwell."

"Yeah," I answered, stronger. "She wants me to help her."

"Fern Caldwell wants you to help her. With what, exactly?" The amused expression was starting to annoy me. He wasn't taking me seriously, that much was obvious.

"I told you. She wants me to help her free King Arthur. By finishing Into the Faraway."

The smug smile melted a bit. "Yes, tell me about that. How do you know the title? We don't release those until just weeks before publication. Nobody outside this office knew about the name of the fourth book. Besides Fern, of course. How did you find out?"

"She told me."

"Who told you?"

"Fern Caldwell!"

"And when exactly did she tell you this?" His tone reeked of skepticism. Wait until he heard my answer.

"Night before last." There was a long, excruciatingly uncomfortable pause before he finally responded.

"Excuse me?"

"It was the night after she died," I explained. "Fern showed up in my bedroom and said she needed my help. She told me the stories were true and that King Arthur could never be free unless the final book was written and published. See, the magic only works when the books are—"

"Stop," Doonesbury snarled. "You're saying Fern Caldwell was in your bedroom night before last?"

"Well, her ghost, her spirit—whatever you want to call it."

Doonesbury looked at me, blankly. "I've heard quite enough codswallop for one day."

My heart sank and my stomach twisted into knots. This wasn't going to work. Disappointed, I got up and headed for the door, stuffing my hands in my pockets for my lucky rock. It sure didn't bring me much luck today. I turned back to plead with Doonesbury one last time and saw the one thing that could save us standing right next to him.

"Oh, wow," I breathed. "She's here. Fern is standing right next to you."

Doonesbury followed my gaze. For a moment, I thought he could see her. His eyes seemed to meet hers. She smiled, sadly. Then she looked at me.

"He doesn't believe you."

I glanced at Colin. His eyes bulged. Could he see her? I wasn't sure.

Fern circled Doonesbury's chair, one hand to her lips in thought. "Tell him I made a copy of the manuscript."

"Um, okay." I looked at Doonesbury. "She wants me to tell you she made a copy of the manuscript."

Doonesbury turned back to me, his eyes narrowing again. "Impossible. She never did that. Never. Craziest thing. Never used a computer either."

Fern huffed, frustrated. "Tell him I made one after the break-in."

"Break-in?" I repeated. Stanley Doonesbury's eyes went from slits to saucers. "She says she made the copy after the break-in," I relayed.

Doonesbury's face shone with sweat. "How do you know about that?" he said, weakly, like maybe he was starting to believe.

"Because she's standing right there telling me!"

"But ... there are no such things as ghosts!"

"Well, apparently there are!"

His expression hardened and he glared at me. "Now listen here, young man, I don't know how you came to learn these things, but I've heard quite enough mumbo-jumbo for one day. Kindly leave."

"Listen, I understand you're scared, I am too, but I need you! I want to help Fern finish the book, but I can't do it by myself. I'm just a kid! Please, you have to help me!"

"I was afraid of this, Henderson," Fern sighed. "He's not a big believer in magic."

"How can he not believe in magic, and be your agent? Fern, help me convince him!" I pleaded with her.

"I'm thinking!" she said, running her hands over her face.

"This is quite enough!" Doonesbury growled, reaching for a button on his desk. "Lindsay, please call security!"

"That won't be necessary, Mr. Doonesbury," Colin said, urgently. "We're going. So sorry to bother you!" Colin grabbed my arm and pulled me toward the door.

Fern snapped her fingers. "I know!" she said. "Tell him about the typewriter. Tell him I have to finish the book on the old Royal."

Colin was pulling me across the floor, but I wrenched my arm free. "Fern said to tell you about the typewriter!" I cried, hoping this would make a difference. "She says the book has to be written on it."

I saw my words hit home, like a switch being flipped; one moment he didn't believe, the next he did.

Relief washed over me and silence fell on the room with a deep hush. Both Colin and I froze, waiting to see the outcome. Then, quietly, Doonesbury spoke. "Good God in Heaven, it's true."

I sighed. "That's what made you believe me?"

"There could have been leaks at the publishing house with the title, but Fern never told anyone about the typewriter and neither did I. Even her official fan site webmasters didn't know. She said her process was private. I kept the secret at her bequest. And I didn't want anyone to steal it. That piece of junk was her talisman, you know. Writers are a superstitious lot." He shook his head.

"So, you'll take me to Glastonbury?" I asked, afraid to hope.

"There is no point." His eyes darted around the room as if looking for Fern. "Because there is no manuscript, nor a copy of it, at her flat. I searched the whole place myself, believe me. Listen, I knew she'd want it published if at all possible. I wasn't even sure how much she'd written. We were meeting to discuss it the day she ...." He paused, frowning. "Even if there was a manuscript, or a copy of it, it wouldn't matter anyway. Not half an hour ago the publisher called to tell me they've hired someone to write the fourth book. A ghost writer," he laughed. "Isn't that ironic?"

"What does that mean?" Colin asked, sounding as stunned as I felt.

"That means, boys, that your beloved Sydney Wakefield series will be concluded after all. It will be published under Fern's name and everyone will think she finished the book before her untimely demise. If they've hired someone decent, no one will know the difference." Doonesbury smiled, looking truly sorry. "Do you have any idea how much money is tied up in these books? Millions of pounds! There's insurance involved. Licensing! Subsidiary rights! The ghostwriter was in her contract—she knew all about it, don't worry yourself over that. I'm sorry she feels so strongly about finishing the story herself that she had to return from the grave to do so, but you'll just have to tell her it just isn't meant to be."

I looked at Fern. She looked stunned. "Fern? Is that true? Can someone else write your books?"

"I suppose it was in the contract somewhere, but I never thought ... " Fern paused and clasped her hands together as if she was praying. "No matter. We have to be the ones to finish the book, Henderson. Another writer won't get it right. They can't get it right, you understand? It has to be us."

I understood. "She has to be the one to finish the book. Or Arthur won't be freed."

Doonesbury sunk back into his chair. "I'm sorry, son. I want to believe you. And her," he gestured to empty air. "But it's out of my hands now. Even if we got the typewriter and the copy of the manuscript, which I don't believe exists, how would I explain our acquisition of it to the publisher?"

"You tell that greedy old coot you found it in my flat!" Fern hollered, although he didn't hear her.

I repeated her words, without the greedy old coot part. Doonesbury shook his head again, sadly. "I promise you, I searched the entire place!"

Fern planted her hands on her hips and smiled mischievously. "Did he look under my knickers drawer?"

"What? Of course I didn't look in there, what do you take me for?" Doonesbury seemed very offended when I passed along Fern's question.

I felt my cheeks grow hot. "She says there's a false bottom where the copy is hidden. The one she made after the break-in."

The little man growled, pursing his lips. "I don't believe it. She was adamant about keeping only the one working manuscript. It was just like writing the darn thing on that old typewriter. Or living in that tiny little flat when she could have afforded a castle!"

I listened to Fern, then relayed her message. "She said she believes in sticking with what works. The first book was written on that typewriter, in that flat. It worked, so she stuck with it. Just like she stuck with you. Now she's asking for your help. Won't you, please? Help her?"

Doonesbury heaved a sigh. "I'm sorry, son. It's just not possible."

"But why not?" I knew I was whining, but I felt my last hope slipping away.

"Things are very busy right now. I have meetings. Work to do. You understand." Doonesbury wouldn't meet my eyes. He shuffled a few papers around on his desk.

Colin's shoulders slumped. He actually seemed disappointed. I looked to Fern for help, but she was fading, and quickly. Before she could get out another word, she was gone.

I heaved a huge sigh. This was beyond not going well, and I was at a loss as to what to do next. "Well, okay then. I can't believe this is all going to end here."

Doonesbury looked up, worry working across his face. Quietly, he said, "Every story must have an ending, young man. And unfortunately, they cannot all be happy ones."

The wrinkled elf looked at them over the crackling fire, his eyes twinkling with the secret, his voice ancient. "Three elements you need to break the curse. Two you have, one you seek."

Bedivere nodded, leaning forward in anticipation. "We have both Excalibur and its Scabbard in our possession. Please, good Fortuna, what is the third element?"

Sydney held her breath. They'd searched so long, and fought so hard to get this far. Was it, finally, time to discover the last piece of the puzzle?

"The Holy Grail."

"The Holy Grail?" Sir Bedivere blurted, dropping his head in defeat. "Impossible. It does not exist!"

"Does it not?" Fortuna smiled with the question. "Not in Camelot, of course, no. Merlin hid it. Far away." Then he looked at Sydney, knowingly. "In your land. It is there you must go. Into the Faraway."

SYDNEY WAKEFIELD
AND THE SWORD HUNTERS

CHAPTER 7

Colin and I walked down Sloane Street. We passed Harrods, avoiding the shoppers coming out with their expensive purchases. Neither of us spoke.

I had the strangest sensation that someone was following us. A shudder rippled through me as I glanced over my shoulder. I saw no one suspicious, just people doing their own things. Still, the feeling clung to me.

My pack was heavy on my back, weighing me down like the burden Fern Caldwell had plopped on my shoulders. I didn't know what to do next. How could I pull this off? I couldn't, that was all there was to it.

I just wanted to go home. I didn't want to be stuck in this crowd of faces, people who didn't know anything about my problem and wouldn't have cared if they did. I glanced back over my shoulder again and this time caught a glimpse of a tall man in a dark cloak. His hood was pulled up against the chill wind, but I caught a glimpse of his eyes beneath it before he looked away. Icy blue. I didn't like the looks of him. I picked up the pace a bit. Colin kept up without commenting, lost in his own thoughts. A few blocks later when I looked back, the stranger was gone.

When we finally reached my place, and Colin collected his bike, I paused. "Thanks for your help today, Colin." I said, with a shrug. "And for believing me."

"Lot of good it did," he muttered, shifting his backpack to his other shoulder.

"It's probably better this way. If Doonesbury had believed me, I would have had to go to Glastonbury, right? Now it's not a choice. There's just no way." I paused. "I still don't know if I even believe this whole thing myself. What if it's just my imagination? Or I'm delusional or something? What if all this is happening just because I don't want to believe Fern Caldwell is dead?"

Colin shuffled his feet, looking at the pavement. "I don't know, HG. I can't tell you what to do. And I can't tell you why, but ... I do think it's real. You're not as mental as you think." He gave me a lopsided grin, and pedaled away.

I plopped down on the cold stone of the front step. I had a ton of homework thanks to evil old. Baines. And I needed to do well on it, given I'd flunked yesterday's quiz that I shouldn't have had to take, since I'd missed class the day before, but Baines shows no mercy.

Studying was the last thing I wanted to do right then. I couldn't stop thinking about what had happened with Doonesbury. About Fern Caldwell. About how I'd failed her.

The air smelled like autumn; the sky, dreary and gray. Clouds hung low and smoky, the blustery wind shoving them through the sky so fast it seemed like one of those time-lapse movies. I closed my eyes, enjoying the misty promise of rain. The L-shaped street of Sloane Gardens, with its tall brownstones on either side, blocked the wind so it wasn't so chilly on my front stoop. I wondered how hot it was back in Texas at the moment. Fall didn't usually arrive there until after November. The colder weather was just one of the things I loved about England. I never could stand heat. I enjoy a good rainy day, and there are plenty of those here.

"I'm back."

I nearly jumped out of my skin. My eyes snapped open. "Jeez! You nearly gave me a heart attack," I snapped, clutching my chest. Fern was coming through really strong this time. She almost looked real, sitting right there next to me on the step.

"Apologies, dear. So, I don't suppose you convinced old Doonesbury to take you to Glastonbury after I faded out on you?"

"No," I said. My mood, which had soared at the sight of her, dropped into the basement again.

She tossed her head defiantly. "No matter. I have another idea. Come on." Fern floated backward through our red front door, sinking through it like water into sand. I grabbed my backpack and dug my key out of the zipper pocket. It wasn't as easy for us mortal folk. We actually had to open the door.

As I shoved the key into the keyhole, I got that oogie feeling again, like I was being watched. I glanced down the street to see that same dark cloaked man I'd seen in front of Harrods's strolling casually down the sidewalk toward me. My heartbeat accelerated into a sprint as I tried to get the key in the lock, but my hands refused to cooperate. C'mon, c'mon! Get the door open!

The key slid and the knob turned and I was inside, throwing the bolt behind me. Big, deep sigh of relief. What was with that guy? Was he really following me? It was probably just a coincidence after all he was going in our direction before, right? Maybe he lived around here.

Shake it off, HG. All this ghost stuff has you spooked.

I double-checked the bolt on the heavy front door and looked up the front staircase as Fern reached the first landing and disappeared around the corner. I detoured into the kitchen to hang my pack on the pantry hook. All the homework inside would have to wait. I grabbed a water bottle from the fridge, loosened my tie and climbed the wooden staircase. As I turned the corner, I nearly ran into Claire.

"Can't you walk without making so much noise? I have homework, you know. And use your headphones if you have to listen to that trash you call music." Claire always complained about me making too much noise, especially after school during homework time. Like she was such the scholar.

"Just because a piece of music was written by someone still living doesn't make it trash," I said. I actually liked the classical music she listened to, but I wasn't going to let on. Besides, I suspected she only listened to it because she thought it made her seem rich or sophisticated or something.

Claire gave me a look, folding her arms menacingly across her chest, blocking my way. I gritted my teeth. Better to pacify her, especially since I needed to get upstairs to Fern. "Don't worry, I'll be quiet. I've got tons of homework. So, don't even think about disturbing me."

Claire glanced at my water bottle as she pushed past me. "I hope that's not the last Evian. You know I'm supposed to drink lots of water."

"There's a whole case of the stuff in there!" Claire had read somewhere about how water was good for your skin and now she acted like some doctor had prescribed her eight bottles a day.

I heard the fridge door open as I shut myself in my bedroom. For about the gazillionth time, I wished I had a lock, but Mom wouldn't allow it. She said it wasn't safe. I think she just wanted free access to my stuff. I don't know what she thought I was hiding. I didn't have any big secrets.

Well, I didn't used to.

Fern Caldwell hovered over my desk chair staring at the cover of Doorway to Avalon again. Her expression was so sad. "Fern?" I said, concerned.

"Oh, hullo." She looked away from the picture and smiled. I relaxed a bit. "Did you ask your sister to take you?" she asked.

I hesitated. "Uh, take me where?"

"To Glastonbury, of course. She has a license, doesn't she?"

"Well, yeah, but we don't have a car ... at least, not here. My mom has it at work." Fern kept acting like it was no big deal for a thirteen-year-old kid to find his way out of London and halfway across England. I wasn't even really sure where Glastonbury was compared to London.

Fern hovered next to my computer. "Do you need a little geography lesson?"

I didn't think I'd ever get used to the mind-reading thing.

Fern smiled and placed one hand on top of the computer monitor. "I never liked these things, but I believe technology might come in a bit handy right now, hmmm?"

Fern watched over my shoulder as I searched for info on Glastonbury. I found a map of the country and could see that the town was west of London, in a part of England called Somerset.

The first website I found told some history of the area. Long ago the ocean had risen up through parts of England, creating marshlands and islands— one of which was the Tor. So that was why the Tor was sometimes called the Island of Avalon. Okay, that made sense.

There were a ton of Glastonbury sites, some about the King Arthur legend and a bunch about a big outdoor concert there, called the Glastonbury Festival. Kind of sounded like that old Woodstock thing I'd heard Mom talk about sometimes.

I saw a few links about the Glastonbury Zodiac, which had something to do with the constellations in the sky matching up with the landscape in that part of England. That sounded cool. I bookmarked those pages so I could go back and read them later. To think that the hills and valleys around Glastonbury were a mirror image of the celestial patterns above them was mind-bending; was it like the stars had stamped themselves on the earth or something? Wicked. I turned to ask Fern if she knew anything about this Zodiac thing, but she was gone again.

Oh, for gosh sakes.

When I looked back at the computer screen, I was surprised to find the website for the First Great Western train company. That was odd. I must have clicked the link by accident.

Could I get to Glastonbury by train? I decided to go ahead and check out the schedule, since I was already on the page and all. The closest station was Castle Cary, but then I'd have to take a taxi into town. I might be able to swing taking a train into the country by myself, but catching a cab all alone? That made me nervous.

Okay, HG. Stop being such a loser. If I was the only one who could help Fern, I was going to have get some guts.

Just as I was screwing up my courage, Claire burst through the door. She wore a blue blouse and skinny jeans. For the millionth time, I couldn't wait until I was old enough to go to the high school. They didn't have to wear school uniforms.

"I need to use your computer," she challenged me, obviously expecting protest. We each got big presents when we moved to England; "guilt gifts" Claire called them. I asked for a totally loaded computer, but Claire wanted a new wardrobe. "What's wrong with your iPad?" Her school gave each student a tablet to use. We didn't get those in our school.

"Battery's dead."

"Well, I'm kinda busy right now," I said, trying to click out of the window before she could see anything.

"Busy with what, surfing all the Sydney Wakefield Reddit threads?" Claire laughed, coming up behind me. She must have caught a glimpse of the train schedule. "Planning on running away. I hope?" she sneered.

"You'd love that, wouldn't you?" I shot right back. "Would you wait a whole minute, or just thirty seconds before snatching up my computer?"

"Nah, I want your room. You know I covet your window seat. Of course, I'd have to get rid of all these infantile books!" Her sneer softened and I thought I saw a brief hint of concern in her eyes. "Seriously, HG, Mom would be wicked corked if you took off. Are you all messed up about Fern Caldwell or what?"

I snorted. "Yeah, searching for me might make Mom miss a meeting."

Claire shook her head. "C'mon, I'm serious, HG. Remember Aunt Maggie?"

Aunt Maggie. I'd thought about her the other night, watching the news coverage of Fern's death.

"I'm not running away," I admitted. "Sorry to disappoint you."

Claire rolled her eyes. "Listen, just because Mom's a total work-monger doesn't mean she wouldn't freak if you vanished."

She was right. And Mom had been pretty great about this whole Fern Caldwell thing. Should I let Claire in on my secret? Fern's suggestion wasn't so bad; Claire did have a driver's license. Barely. If we could just find some wheels. But doubtful that she'd believe me. If she did, I wouldn't have to take the train by myself. Or a cab. Doonesbury wasn't going to be any help, and I sure couldn't ask Mom. Maybe Claire really was the only option.

I had to give her a try.

"Why are you looking at me like that?" Claire asked, hands on her hips. "HG, what weirdness is going on with you?"

"Claire," I sighed, "you'd better sit down. Because what's going on is most definitely weird."

Modred was furious. He stood on the battlement, his smoldering eyes burning holes in the mists gathering over the moor. His men had failed to capture the girl and Bedivere, and now the Scabbard was gone as well. How the scourge had managed to not only get into the castle but into his mother's chambers to find their precious talisman, Modred couldn't imagine.

His mother was still bleary-eyed from whatever potion they'd used on her—she couldn't remember a thing. The separation from the Scabbard wasn't helping. He sensed time inching its way through his veins, the years bleeding from him like an open wound. He had to locate these traitors, and soon. If he didn't, he and his mother would die. And if that happened, Avalon would be sure to follow.

SYDNEY WAKEFIELD
AND THE SWORD HUNTERS

CHAPTER 8

I had to give Claire credit. She didn't laugh.

I thought she would, I mean, who wouldn't? I even laughed as I was re-telling the darn story, it sounded so wonky, like Colin would say. But her eyes kept getting wider and rounder.

When I finished, I dropped my head into my hands and stared at the floor. "Go ahead, call me mental."

Claire called me just that, and regularly, but this time she was completely silent. It was too odd. I looked up from my hands, thinking she might have just left me sitting there. But she hadn't moved. "Why aren't you ripping into me?" I demanded.

Without answering, she did exactly what I'd thought, and walked out of the room. I knew she would just bail on me. Then she was back, a piece of paper in her hand. Actually, two pieces of paper, folded in half. She handed them to me.

I got a strange feeling that the weirdness needle on this whole situation was about to peg red. "What is this?" I asked, unfolding the papers, not sure I really wanted to know.

"Just look," Claire said, and her voice trembled. My stomach tightened. This couldn't be good. It took a lot to rattle Claire.

The first page was a computer printout from one of those online mapping engines. I remembered Mom had printed out something like this once when we took a road trip to Oxford one weekend. This one showed the southwest section of England. The route between London to Glastonbury was highlighted with a bright purple line. The second sheet of paper was driving directions from London to Glastonbury's High Street, including a detailed street map of Glastonbury itself with a star smack in the middle of High Street. I looked up at the top of the page where it listed the departure coordinates and my heart just about stopped.

The directions were from our home address.

"Where did you get this?" I breathed.

"It was tucked inside a book." Claire crossed her arms, hugging herself.

I stopped, considering. "You don't think that I—"

"No," Claire shook her head, eyes wide in amazement. "I don't. They weren't there yesterday. I pulled it out of my backpack at lunch today, to catch up on my assigned reading. These papers were tucked inside the front cover."

"Like, can that even be a coincidence?" Could Fern have done it somehow? But how? She said herself how computer illiterate she was. And how would she have put it in the book? I didn't think she could affect the physical world like that, at least, it didn't seem like it. If she could, she'd just write the darn book herself. No, it couldn't have been her.

"That's not the craziest part," Claire said, rubbing her eyes wearily.

"What is?" I asked, afraid for what she would say.

"My lit book, the one I found this in? Le Morte d'Arthur by Sir Thomas Malory. Ever heard of it?"

Had I heard of it?

"It's only the most famous book ever written about King Arthur," I whispered.

"Exactly. It's almost like ..."

"A sign," I completed her thought.

"Yeah," she agreed.

"So, then, you believe me?" I ventured.

Claire's eyes glazed over, resigned. "I don't know if I believe you have been conversing with a ghost or anything, but I sure think this whole map thing has to be more than a strange coincidence."

I took a deep breath, relief flooding through me. "Well, I don't know who put those papers in your book, but I'm grateful they did. Because you are my way to Glastonbury."

Claire sank onto my bed. "But how am I going to help you do that? It's not like I have my own car or anything."

"What about Becca? Doesn't she have a Mini?" Becca was Claire's best friend. She'd just turned eighteen and her dad owned some big company so they had serious money.

"I suppose I could ask her, but how would I explain it? I can't exactly tell her why we need to go to Glastonbury, can I?"

"You don't think she'd believe you?" I asked, sarcastically. Claire was right, this was hopeless. And then, a miracle happened.

Mom came home.

I looked up and saw her standing in my bedroom doorway. I jumped, wondering how much of our conversation she'd heard.

"Mom?" Claire said. Mom didn't respond. "Hey, are you okay?"

Claire was right to ask, because Mom did look really strange. She was swaying back and forth, and her face was a weird, pale color. Then she let out an enormous sneeze. "'Scuze me," she moaned, putting one hand to her forehead. I glanced at my desk clock. It was only 3:30.

"Not feeling well. Thought I'd better get some rest. Boss insisted I come home. I'm okay …" Mom's briefcase slipped from her hands and bounced to the floor as she turned and headed for her bedroom. Claire and I exchanged looks before following her down the hall.

"Stay back, I think I have the flu," she muttered, shedding clothing with each step. By the time she reached the bed, she was down to her blouse and underwear. She collapsed onto the mattress, pulling a throw blanket over her. Claire ignored Mom's warning and followed her to the bed, touching her forehead.

"She's burning up," Claire whispered. "Go grab some water." When I returned from the kitchen with another Evian, Claire had Mom sitting up and popping Tylenol in her mouth.

I handed her the water which she gulped down, then sunk back into the pillows. Claire had gotten her under the covers while I was gone, too.

We left her there to sleep, and Claire gave me a curious look as she pulled her bedroom door shut. I couldn't remember the last time Mom had gotten sick. And while I was concerned about my mother's health, my conniving little brain couldn't help plotting.

I moved down the hall to where my mom's briefcase lay on the floor. Looking back at Claire, I couldn't stop my mouth from turning up into a smile.

"I can not believe I let you talk me into this. We're going to get lost. Or arrested!" Claire steered the Renault off the M25 motorway and onto the M3. I relaxed a bit. We'd survived the most difficult part—getting out of London. Now we just had to find our way through the English countryside.

"Don't worry. It's all good." Easy for me to say. I wasn't the one driving my mother's car, although I was most certainly an accomplice. I wondered how much jail time that would get me.

Despite her saying she didn't believe the printed-out directions were a coincidence, it hadn't been easy convincing Claire to take Mom's keys. We both were brought up to know right from wrong, and stealing was most definitely wrong, especially from family members. But Mom wasn't going to just let us take the car, was she? And sure, she was sick, but she just needed some sleep and Tylenol. And while she was doing that, why couldn't we take a little jaunt out to Glastonbury?

It would take us a little over three hours to get there according to the anonymously provided directions. I grabbed the car keys from Mom's briefcase and broke into my piggy bank. Combined with Claire's secret cash stash (which she was now irritated I knew about), we had about 200 pounds between us. I figured we could be in Glastonbury by 7 o'clock, get the manuscript out of Fern's drawer, grab Fern's special typewriter, and be home before morning. Mom would probably sleep the whole time.

We left a note just in case she woke up, telling her we'd gone out for pizza. Hopefully, she'd just go back to bed and not text us or anything. We'd both turned off the locations on our phone, in case she tried to track us.

Claire heaved another huge sigh, something she'd been doing frequently ever since we got in the car. I hoped she would cut it out now that we'd made it to the M3. It was really getting on my nerves.

She'd learned how to drive the "English" way, meaning on the opposite side of the road from how they drive in America. She'd only had her license for two months, so it was all she knew, but this was her first big road trip. She was understandably nervous. Claire was using a GPS app to guide us, but I'd brought the paper print out along anyway.

The weather out here in the countryside was an improvement over London. Warm sunshine illuminated the lush sheep pastures on either side of the road. Every once in a while, we'd pass a quaint little town. Almost all of them had some old church complete with tall steeples. The forest grew thick in spots, wearing a full range of autumn colors to announce the arrival of the season. I wondered how long the reds and oranges and purples would last this year. Usually, rain and wind stole the trees' beauty and created a mushy brown mess that we had to walk through until the first snowfall. But at this point, the colors were just beginning to show.

I glanced over at the speedometer. Claire was keeping it around 90 kph, which wasn't too much over the posted limit, but I told her to slow down anyway. We couldn't get pulled over. My speed-demon sister sighed. Again. "I can't believe we're doing this. This better be the real thing, HG. I'd better not have risked losing my license and getting grounded for the rest of my life for nothing. Seriously. That's all I'm saying." She sounded grumpy, but underneath I thought I detected a hint of excitement.

Without responding, since she'd said the same thing a dozen times already, I leaned over and pushed the "On" button on the radio. I needed something to keep us pumped. Mom had the satellite station on 90s Jam, which was okay by me. I leaned my head against the window and spun my lucky rock in my palm to the beat of Holiday by Green Day, until Claire pointed out a road sign. "Look! Stonehenge! I've always wanted to see that."

I glanced at Claire's phone in the dash mount as the clipped British voice of the GPS hadn't updated us on our progress in a while. "Looks like our exit is coming up." I tucked the rock safely back in my jeans.

The rest of the route continued along smaller two-lane roads that wound on and on through the countryside. Unfortunately, they were so narrow Claire couldn't go as fast. Oncoming traffic zipped by my window at stomach-turning speeds. Claire's tension grew, her knuckles white at ten and two on the steering wheel. I was relieved when we finally reached the turn toward Pilton. According to the arrival time on the app, we were almost there.

"That bookstore better still be open," Claire murmured and my heart stopped beating for a moment. She had a point. It'd be almost seven o'clock by time we arrived. What if the store was closed? How would we find Franklin Temple then? Panic simmered in my stomach.

"Can you hurry?" I said, unable to hide the tremble in my voice. "Franklin Temple, Fern's neighbor, is the guy who runs the store. He's the one with the key to Fern's flat."

"You told me to stick to the speed limit. And what do we do if he's not there?" Claire asked, glaring at me.

"Just keep your eyes on the road, okay? We'll find him. Besides, Fern will show up once we get to Glastonbury. I know she will."

"She already has," said a voice from the backseat. I whirled around to see a familiar ghost.

Claire just about ran the car off the road. Shrubbery scraped against the side of the car as she regained control. "Oh wow, oh wow, oh holy wow. HG! I heard her." She tentatively glanced in the rearview mirror. Fern wiggled her fingers in greeting. "I can see her, too! This can't be real. Fern Caldwell is in my car!"

I grinned. "Hi, Fern. I was hoping you'd show up."

"Well, you're close to Glastonbury now, and that seems to make me stronger. It's been said, you know, that strange forces are at work around here. Anything can happen."

That reminded me. "Hey, Fern, did you put the map in Claire's Lit book?"

"Map? I'm sorry, I don't know what you're talking about."

"Someone printed out a map with directions to Glastonbury and tucked it inside one of Claire's books. A book about King Arthur. That's why she believed me this afternoon when I asked her to bring me out here. I thought it might have been you, trying to help convince her."

Fern's eyes narrowed. "What was the name of the book?" she asked.

"*Le Morte d'Arthur*," Claire answered, slowing as another car approached going the opposite direction. "By Thomas Malory."

Fern's expression darkened. "Hmmm. That is strange. Yes, indeed it is."

"We couldn't believe it was just a coincidence."

"No, I can't imagine that." Fern twirled a lock of hair through her fingers, deep in thought. "I, for one, don't believe in coincidences." Fern thought for a moment. "*Le Morte d'Arthur*. Do you know the English translation?"

I felt Claire tense beside me, as if she never made the connection before.

"*Le Morte d'Arthur*," Claire repeated. "The death of Arthur."

The barge moved silently through the dark waters toward the island, the shallow boat barely making a ripple, as if floating across glass. The night was so deep and moonless, Sydney could not see the Tor above them, but she could sense its towering presence.

A tear stole from Sydney's eye and slipped down her cheek. She hadn't made a sound, but Gavin appeared beside her to wipe the tear away.

"It's too much," Sydney choked through her tears. "I'm not meant for great things like this."

Gavin cocked his head in question. "But, of course you are. You must be," he said, so certain that Sydney almost could believe it herself.

"How can you be so sure?" she asked, desperate for his confidence.

"It's simple. Merlin was waiting. And the one who came was you."

SYDNEY WAKEFIELD
AND THE SWORD HUNTERS

Chapter 9

I caught my first glance of the Tor and St. Michael's Tower as we rounded a corner. The lush, green hill loomed, thick with grass, the evening sky turning purple behind it. Red and yellow trees gathered at its base like worshippers at an altar. The Tower stuck off its top, looking like a forgotten domino. It was an eerie site, this hill hovering over the rooftops of the little town, like a giant ready to pounce.

"Whoa," I breathed. "There's the Tor."

"I'm afraid to look at it. I can't take my eyes off the road," Claire complained. "These lanes are ridiculously narrow! And these people drive like maniacs!" Claire braked as another car went by going the other way.

"Imagine what the Tor must have looked like all those many years ago," Fern mused from the backseat. "When most of this land was swamp, a huge church perched at the summit."

"Was that tower part of it?" asked Claire, glancing quickly up at the hill.

"No, the original church built there was a monastery, but it was destroyed by an earthquake on September 11th, 1275. St. Michael's Tower was probably built a hundred or so years later."

"A monastery … is that St. Joseph's from Secret of the Tor?" I said, excited. "The place where they find the entrance to the tunnels beneath the Dark Avalon's Tor."

Fern chuckled. "You are quite the expert on these books, Henderson Green. It's no wonder I'm able to appear to you."

We rode along in silence for a moment. I saw glimpses of the Tower atop the Tor between clumps of trees zipping past the window.

The next thing I knew, we were turning onto High Street.

People milled about on the sidewalks. A number of stores were obviously named for the town's mystical connection: Avalon Shoes, The Speaking Tree, The Psychic Piglet, but there were also ordinary bakeries, newsstands, and banks. Many had colorful banners and awnings. On some blocks, the buildings seemed very old; others were obviously newer. As the road veered left, I saw a plaza to our right, a host of green café tables and chair standing empty around a stone spire. It looked like a buried church was trying to push its way up through the ground.

The GPS voice told us our destination was ahead on the left, just this side of an elegant cathedral, its spires stretched toward the darkening sky. Bells pealed as if to announce our arrival. Seven o'clock, on the dot.

Fern pointed to the right side of the street where two cars were parked: a battered old Jeep with a tattered, canvas roof, and a slick, red Porsche roadster. "How interesting. That's Doonesbury's car."

Claire pulled into the empty space behind the Porsche. "Isn't Doonesbury the guy you went to see, HG?" Claire asked as she shifted the Renault into PARK.

"Yep. He's Fern's agent." I got out of the car and immediately was struck by the spicy, woody scent of the air. It reminded me of the candles Mom liked. I felt a sudden pang of guilt, thinking about her lying sick in her bed at home, not knowing her children were miles away and in the company of a ghost.

Fern appeared at my side. I realized she wasn't much taller than me, and that when her feet hovered near the ground, we actually saw eye to eye. "Why do you think Doonesbury is here?" I asked her.

"Only one reason I can imagine," Fern growled. "I suspect he's decided to dig through my knickers."

The setting sun painted everything in a fiery light. I pulled my uniform jacket closed and buttoned it up against the chilly air as we crossed the street. I wished I'd taken the time to throw on a sweatshirt and jeans before we'd left. Claire had put on a black sweater over her blouse, and the cold didn't seem to bother her.

Movement near the plaza caught my eye, and I thought I saw someone wearing a dark-colored cloak near that strange spire. I looked at Fern, to see if she'd noticed, but she was already beside the building. When I turned back to the plaza, it was empty. Must have been my imagination.

"This is it," Fern said, glancing up at the second story. Then she disappeared. A placard hanging over our heads read: The Chalice Bookstore. My heartbeat kicked up a notch. It looked just the way it had in the Doorway to Avalon movie. Even though we were on a very important mission, and I wasn't sure what was going to happen, I couldn't help the excitement I felt. I was in Glastonbury! The town where my favorite stories of all time began—both literally and fictionally. How cool!

The bookstore was on the first floor of a building that nestled right next to the arched stone-way of the Glastonbury Abbey Gate. The first-floor exterior of the shop was painted white while the second and third floors above the shop were bricked, with the windows outlined in pale stone. The second and third floors must be Franklin's and Fern's flats.

I cupped my hands around my eyes and peered through the front window. It was a cozy store with wooden floors and every inch of wall space covered with bookshelves. Scattered around the room were display tables. In the front window was a display holding numerous Sydney Wakefield books, as well as one called Finding Avalon through the Eye of the Crystal.

I didn't see any people inside, though. Claire tapped my shoulder and pointed to a sign notifying us that The Chalice Bookstore was CLOSED, PLEASE CALL AGAIN. "I knew this was going to happen!" she barked.

"Oh man!" I moaned. "Now what are we going to do?"

Voices rang out above us. Claire and I stepped back from the door, searching for the source of the sound, which appeared to be the open second story window.

"You don't understand, old man, I'm trying to help!" It sounded like Doonesbury.

"Well, she doesn't quite see it that way," replied a calm, much older voice.

"This was her dream, to finish the story. You know that! Will you deny her that last wish?"

Claire looked at me, questioning. "The younger one is definitely Doonesbury," I said. The older man must be Franklin Temple.

"I'm sorry you drove all the way out here for nothing, but she doesn't want you to have it," the man I assumed to be Franklin said.

"And how do you know that?"

"Because she just told me. And if you don't believe me, ask her yourself. She's standing right behind you."

Claire and I glanced at each other and sniggered. I could imagine Doonesbury freaking out after being told once again that his most famous client was a ghost. There was a loud thump, then a face appeared at the window.

"Be down to let you two in momentarily," called the old man.

A few seconds later, a door just to the left of the shop's front door opened and Franklin Temple welcomed us inside. He wore his white hair pulled back into a ponytail; a loose, long-sleeved purple shirt covered with paisleys; and baggy green pants that didn't quite reach his bare feet. He smiled at us with dark brown eyes that sparkled with mischief. Mom probably would have called him a hippy. "Come in, come in. Fern said you were here! I'm most pleased to see her, and to meet you!"

We entered the hallway behind him and found a staircase that led to a landing where another set of stairs snaked up to the third floor. The door to the second-floor flat was open, and Franklin ushered us inside. Doonesbury lay crumpled on the floor next to a small kitchen table.

"Is he okay?" Claire asked, inspecting him cautiously as if he were a sleeping snake that might wake and bite her without warning.

"Don't mind Mr. Doonesbury," Franklin said, waving his hand at the unconscious agent. "He received quite a shock. I expect he didn't really believe in spirits until today."

I looked around the sparsely decorated flat. On the front wall, three tall windows overlooked the square. An enormous, overstuffed recliner stood by the farthest right window. Next to it, a side table with a lamp shaped like a thick tree with gnarled branches that reached up into a shade instead of a canopy of leaves. On the other side of the easy chair, taking up most of the wall, was an enormous brick fireplace with a few framed photographs on the mantle.

"Now then, we haven't been properly introduced. I am Franklin Temple. Fern says you are Henderson Green." He held out his hand to me and I shook it.

"Yes, sir. And this is my sister, Claire."

"Of course it is. My dear, it is a pleasure."

Claire smiled, awkwardly. I quickly asked, "Where did Fern go?"

"Upstairs," Franklin said. He sank into a high-back chair and removed a pipe from the stand on the side table. Striking a match, he poked it into the bowl of his pipe and sucked deeply at the other end. The smoke circled up creating shapes that looked strangely like soft-edged stars. On the wall behind Franklin's chair, a cuckoo clock played a little song to let us know it was 7:15.

"Mr. Temple," I began, "did Fern tell you why she asked me to come here?"

He took a long pull on his pipe, blowing the smoke toward the open window where most of it sailed off into the night. It smelled as sweet as the air outside. I was feeling very calm all of a sudden, and as Claire sunk into a ragged couch against the far wall, it looked as if she might be feeling much the same way.

"Yes, dear boy, she told me. You are here because powers greater than we can understand have chosen you to help Fern finish what has been started. Despite her … situation." Franklin's eyes twinkled but his expression was serious.

"Great, then you can help me find the manuscript and Fern's typewriter. We really should be getting back to London before my mom realizes we're
gone—"

"Oh no, you can't go yet," the old man said. "We need you here. In Glastonbury."

"But we can't stay," I sputtered, putting out my hands as if to stop a train from running me down. "We've got to get back! My mom is—"

"I realize the difficulties this will cause, Henderson Green," Franklin interrupted again. "But there are bigger problems at hand here. Lives are at stake. Mortal and spiritual. And, a prophecy waits to be fulfilled. A prophecy in which you play a very large part."

"But I don't think—"

"Then don't think, dear boy. Just do. Do what is right. Do what your heart says you must. Free Arthur. And in doing so, save someone else. Someone very precious to me. My grand-daughter, Sydney."

CHAPTER 10

I sank down onto the couch next to Claire. The fabric was worn with age and mottled with snags. It looked how I felt.

And then it hit me. Why hadn't I thought of this before?

"Near the end of Sword Hunters, Sydney and Sir Bedivere are trying to escape Dark Avalon to come back to present day Glastonbury to find the Holy Grail." At the beginning of the last chapter, the only part I'd read, Sydney and Bedivere waited in the woods for sunset, for just the right time to get to the Living Rock in Dark Avalon, and open the Doorway. "Isn't that what happens at the end of the book?"

"Yes, but when they get to Sydney's flat," Claire paused, and looked at Franklin, worried. "They find her grandfather on the floor, unconscious."

The only one unconscious at the moment was Doonesbury. Then I jolted as I realized what Claire had just said. I turned to her, my mouth gaping.

"Wait, you read it?" I was speechless.

Claire looked sheepish. "Okay, Becca let me borrow hers. I didn't tell you about it because I knew you'd think it meant something, and it didn't." She looked at Fern, apologetically. "At least, it didn't at the time."

I shook my head, trying to clear the fuzzy disbelief from between my ears. "We'll talk about this later," I growled, sounding like my mother. "All right then, what happens after they find Franklin?"

"Nothing," Claire looked back and forth between Franklin and me. "We still don't know why he's unconscious and the book ends with

Bedivere promising Sydney that when they find the Grail, they'll be able to save both Arthur and Sydney's grandfather."

"That doesn't make sense, though. Fern said that everything that takes place in the books takes place in real life. But if that's true, then why isn't Sydney here? And Bedivere? And why aren't you on the floor like him?" I motioned toward Doonesbury.

"Those are questions Fern and I have been wondering for months," said Franklin as a puzzled expression crossed his face. He leaned forward, studying me. "But I don't understand. Have you not read this book?"

"Of course, I've read it!" I protested, rubbing my eyes with the heels of my hands. "Just ... not the last chapter," I sighed.

"Not the last chapter," Franklin murmured, leaning back in his chair and fixing me with a piercing gaze. "Interesting." He was tugging on his beard, lost in thought.

"What's got you so contemplative?" came the soft voice and I whipped around to find Fern's ghost standing in the doorway. Like she needed a door.

"Your friend Henderson here," Franklin said thoughtfully, rocking back and forth. "Did you know he hasn't finished the last chapter of Sword Hunters?"

Fern said nothing for a moment, and then Franklin's words seemed to sink in. "Oh, my goodness," she gasped. One hand fluttered to her mouth. "Do you think it could be possible?"

"I think it's more than possible," he answered with a smile, his eyes shining.

"What are you talking about?" I asked cautiously, not sure I wanted to hear the answer.

"What about a test?" Fern nearly bubbled over with enthusiasm. "Let's see if you're right." She moved into the room, closer to Franklin. "You see, children, we've been waiting all summer for Sydney to appear. We were positive that once Sword Hunters came out and was read, Sydney would come home. But it never happened. I couldn't understand it. Obviously, many readers had finished the book. So why hadn't the events written come to pass?"

"Can I ask a question?" Claire interjected, half raising her hand to interrupt. "Why are you so positive everything in the books is really happening? How can you know that Avalon is even real? I mean, it seems like all you really know is that Sydney disappeared. Since she hasn't returned like in the book, doesn't that kind of prove that she was just kidnapped or something? I mean, someone who knew she was the namesake for the character could have taken her just for that reason. That would still be terrible, obviously …" Claire paused, swallowed, and then said what she was thinking. "My point is: doesn't the fact that she hasn't returned kind of disprove everything you're saying? You know, other than the fact that you're a ghost and all. And we all can see you and hear you. Other than that."

Franklin pushed himself out of his easy chair and went to the bookshelf beside the front window. "Sometimes, my fair lady, proof is not always black and white. We do know everything happening in the books is playing out in Avalon." He searched the shelves, then pulled down a book I immediately recognized as Sword Hunters. He walked over to me, handed me the book, and smiled at Claire. "Because of the dreams," he said, wiggling his gray eyebrows. Then he headed toward the kitchen. "Anyone for some tea? I've got Chamomile."

"Dreams? But, how do dreams prove anything?" asked Claire.

Fern's smile was patient. "Henderson knows what kind of dreams Franklin is talking about."

This silenced Claire for a moment. I didn't think she knew about my dreams, but the look on her face told me differently. Had Mom told her?

"Claire," I asked. "Did Mom ever say anything to you about me after, uhm, Grandma died?"

She put her hands to her face, covering it for a second, before she pulled them away and looked at me. There were tears in her eyes. "HG, that wasn't real."

"Really? After seeing a ghost and being part of a rescue party to save King Arthur, a few psychic dreams shouldn't freak you out."

"I'm not freaked," Claire squeaked, swallowing hard. "So, tell me about the dreams."

"Fern told me the other night. She should tell you."

Fern floated over to the window, her expression distant as she went through the whole thing, explaining it all again.

"So," Claire said when she was done, "Arthur was, like, helping you write the stories."

"Yes, he's playing a big part in his own rescue," Fern smiled. "But what Franklin and I have just realized, is that Henderson may play just as big a part as Arthur or even Sydney. In fact, you very well may play the biggest part of all."

"Wait, what? Me?" My throat closed up and I felt as if my head had been frozen inside an ice cube.

"Open up that book, son." Franklin moved to the kitchen and turned on a gas burner on the stove. As I opened the well-read book and flipped through the front pages, he filled the kettle and plunked it on the flame.

"There," Fern said, looking over my shoulder.

I read aloud. "To my dedicated readers, you have my deepest gratitude for giving my stories a life they would never have, but for your faithfulness."

"I think we were wrong. I think the only dedicated reader having an effect on this story," Franklin said, taking three red mugs down from the white cupboard, "is you, Henderson."

My heart nearly stopped. What was he talking about?

"I think it's possible that you are the one bringing the stories to life," Fern whispered.

I was stunned.

"No, that can't be."

"Oh, yes it can," Fern chirped with excitement. "I don't know why I didn't figure it out before now. Think about it."

My head felt like someone had filled it with cement. "No, I don't want to think about it."

"How many millions of people have read Sword Hunters, and yet Sydney hasn't come back. You, who are obviously connected to this story in other ways, have read every word of every story, multiple times even. All but that last chapter. Sydney hasn't returned because you haven't read about her coming back."

We all sat there for a minute, silently contemplating this. And then Claire had to shoot her mouth off and make me feel horrible.

"He would have finished it by now if he didn't draw the whole thing out so darn long!" Claire growled. "And then there's this stay- up-and-read-the-last-chapter-at-midnight thing."

"Hold it, hold it," I said, closing my eyes tightly. "This is mental! It can't be that my reading the stories brings them to life. It just can't." I looked at Claire, then back at Franklin. "Can it?"

Before anyone could answer, we heard a moan from the floor and Stanley Doonesbury sat up, holding a hand to his forehead. He groaned, looking around. "Hullo? What just happened?"

"You fainted dead away, chap," Franklin chuckled.

"I guess I gave you quite a shock, Stanley. Sorry about that," Fern said, leaning around me.

"Good Lord, it is you!" he gasped, clutching at his chest as if he could convince his heart to keep beating despite the shock. "You're alive!"

"Well, you're partly correct," Fern responded, crossing her arms. "It's me, but no, I am not alive. One question remains to be answered, however. Why are you here, Stanley?"

His awed expression darkened as he saw me. "What's this?" he asked, ignoring Fern's question. "I thought you said you couldn't get here without me."

"This is my sister, Claire," I said. "She drove me down this afternoon."

"Well, aren't you the resourceful one."

"You refused to help me, Mr. Doonesbury."

"Yes, well, after you left my office, I got to thinking. I had to check, just in case there really was a copy. Even if Fern hadn't finished the story, the ghostwriter would have a beginning to work from, and there would be something of Fern in the final book. Today was my first chance to drive over. But he," Doonesbury looked pointedly at Franklin, "won't let me into her flat."

Doonesbury pushed himself up from the floor and stomped his feet, as if trying to get the blood circulating in his legs. "What are you hiding, old man?"

"I'm not the one with anything to hide, am I?" Franklin growled, accusingly.

Fern floated across the room to the window and looked out. "Everyone calm down. I do believe Stanley has my best interests at heart. And now that he can see that I am, indeed, here, he will do everything he can to help us complete the book, the right way. You won't let the ghost writer do it, will you, Stanley?"

Doonesbury paused, a deep flush crawling up his neck. "Of course not. No ghost writers, except for you. I'll help however I can, of course. I owe you my career, my dear."

"Indeed," Franklin muttered, putting the mugs on a tray. He'd set out a tin of biscuits and some sliced cheese. My stomach rumbled. "Tea anyone? I realize it's a bit past tea time," Franklin said, sarcastically. "As a matter of fact, Henderson, you'd better get reading. It's nearly sundown." He carried it into the main room and set it on the coffee table.

"I'm still not sure I believe all this is my doing."

"What's all his doing?" Doonesbury grabbed a piece of cheese and nibbled on it.

"We believe that it's Henderson's reading of the books that's making them come true," explained Franklin.

"But he hasn't finished the last chapter yet," Claire added.

Doonesbury's eyes grew wide. "I take it Henderson doesn't agree?"

"I don't know what to think," I said. The book was heavy in my hands.

"Well, that makes two of us," Doonesbury said and shook his head. "Read away, and if Sydney shows up, then we'll all know for sure. Right?"

I hesitated. "I suppose …"

"Wait!" Claire said, as I flipped the book open to the last chapter. "I've been thinking about something."

We all looked at her, expectantly. "You can't finish the book just yet," she said.

"Why not?" Franklin asked as the teakettle finally whistled.

"Something will happen to Mr. Temple. Remember? Sydney and Bedivere find her grandfather lying unconscious on the floor. Obviously, he's not unconscious now. So, if your theory is correct, once Henderson reads the book, whatever happens to make him unconscious will … happen."

As we thought about that, Franklin spoke. "No matter, and please Claire, call me Franklin. I appreciate your concern for my welfare, but Henderson must read, and quickly. There are reasons for everything, child, reasons that are not always apparent at first. What happens in the book has purpose. When or if that purpose is revealed is up to Fern. And, Arthur. And, I suppose, the powers that be."

"Wait, Claire is right," I broke in. "I don't want to do anything that's going to hurt Mr. Temple … Franklin. What if," I thought for moment then clung to a hope. "What if we changed it? Could we re-write the ending?"

Fern's expression looked sad. "I know it's hard to understand right now, Henderson, but everything needs to happen the way it does in the book. I can't explain any more than that. But trust me when I tell you everything will be okay. Franklin will come through this just fine."

I heaved a sigh and picked up the book from the table. I supposed I had to trust her. I felt clueless, like a pawn being moved around a chess board without knowing the whole game plan. Claire looked at me and I could tell she was thinking about Franklin. I was, too.

But it seemed I had no choice. I took the book to the couch, opened it to Chapter 24, and began to read.

PART TWO

Sydney Wakefield and the Sword Hunters
by Fern Caldwell

Chapter Twenty Four

The castle guards had spotted them. How had they seen them, the woods were so thick, and the cloudy evening so dark? Sydney couldn't imagine, but somehow, they had.

A trumpet blared out a warning. "We must go!" Bedivere grabbed her arm, yanking her back toward the horses, helping her onto the back of the white mare. A single kick was all it took, and they were running. The regal steed surged out of the forest cover, its hooves pounding the earth with mighty speed.

Bedivere's horse kept pace and the two raced across the valley, side by side. The jeweled hilt of Excalibur peeked from the Scabbard strapped across Bedivere's hip, glittering majestically. She prayed they'd make it to the Rock without a fight, but their pursuers sounded much too close.

The sun, sinking ever closer to the crests of the western hills, emerged from a bank of dark clouds, its light streaming angrily toward the castle high on its protective hill.

"There they are!"

Sydney followed Bedivere's gaze, her heart leaping with renewed hope. To the south, a dozen riders had emerged onto the plain, all outfitted in full armor. The front rider carried a flag which bore the familiar crest of a red dragon.

Arthur's crest.

"The Knights!" Sydney exclaimed. Sydney thought they'd never see them again. "But how did they know we were here?"

"Do not question good fortune! Follow me!" Bedivere hollered, reining his horse to the right. "There is not much time!"

How right he was. They had to touch the Rock right at sunset to open the Doorway, or at least that's how it had worked before. It seemed she had just come to terms with believing she was really here, in

Morgan's Dark Avalon, and now she had to leave it behind. But it wouldn't be for long. Once they found the Grail back home in Glastonbury, they would return to free Arthur. They were so close to having all the elements needed to awaken him. But while they'd come far in their quest, Sydney feared the most difficult challenges might still lie ahead.

The castle loomed above, aglow in the blazing orange light of the setting sun. Her eyes absorbed its unearthly beauty, knowing the structure was as false as its current ruler.

"I'll be back, Arthur," she whispered. "I'll be back with the means to save you."

Determined, Sydney turned to face the task ahead and fixed her gaze on the Rock.

The Rock that would take her home.

Unblemished and complete, the Rock sat at the base of the hill fort, mirroring its present-day counterpart at the base of the Tor. It was so different from the primordial remnants she had touched to open the Doorway in her world.

Sydney heard the clash as the Knights intercepted the guards, and said a quick prayer for the safety of those names she'd once only read about in books: Sir Ector, Sir Clarrus, Sir Bors …

"Sydney!" Bedivere warned, and Sydney behind them to see a band of guards split from the main group, and continue their pursuit.

The Rock was still an achingly long distance off. The mare was foaming with sweat, her breathing labored with fatigue. Sydney hugged the satiny white neck tightly. "We're almost there, girl."

They would make it. They would reach the Rock first, if only by a hair. God forbid the magic didn't work … nothing else would matter then.

Bedivere jumped first, pulling back harshly on the reins and leaping from the saddle. Sydney leaned back at once, tugging the leather straps to her chest. "Whoa!!" she yelled.

The mare dug her hooves into the dirt and skidded to a stop. Bedivere pulled Sydney to the ground and the two of them ran the last few steps, hand in hand. "Here they come!" Bedivere cried, sliding Excalibur from its sheath without letting go of her hand. It glinted in the dying light.

As soon as she saw Excalibur's protective sheen, Sydney knew they would make it. And just before she felt the hard stone beneath her fingers, a laugh bubbled up from her chest.

Home.

She was going home!

The Living Rock. Strange how something of such significance could, with the passage of so much time, become a crumbling tourist attraction marked by a weathered, rickety bench. Here, the stone was still inscribed with the words long worn away on its 21st century side.

Forever Avalon.

Morgan's plan for eternal misery and tyranny.

Sydney remembered what the great elf Fortuna had said—by turning a holy place like this into a perpetual prison, Morgan had permanently tarnished her magic; the mists of her betrayal doomed to hover in the sky, a haze of time that embraced the stone walls. It was a curse, fragile only for that split second each day when the sun crossed the horizon.

For an instant, The Rock was cold against her palm. Then she felt the warm vibration, as if the stone welcomed her back.

A bank of mist immediately collected before them, the Doorway slowly appearing within its folds. "Hurry, hurry!" Sydney urged. The Doorway looked much the same as it had from the other side: a gaping maw ripped in the fabric of time and space, shimmering as it magically opened.

The ground began to tremble. The rumbling grew—a crescendo of sound that, although would lead to her salvation, was terrifying in its intensity.

"Go! Now!" Bedivere shouted, holding his shield over Sydney as an arrow careened off its polished surface.

Sydney ran like she had never run before, with speed fueled by fear and the zinging sound of arrows sailing through the air. She and Bedivere raced across the grass toward the beckoning split, plunging through the thick, heavy cavity of the gap. It closed behind them with a sizzling zip.

Dark Avalon was gone. Sydney tripped over the concrete footpath and tumbled into the grass. Bedivere did the same, rolling toward a cluster of trees. Gasping in relief and shock, Sydney looked up the Tor toward St. Michael's Tower. It was good to see the familiar landmark back in its rightful place. In Avalon, the Tor was crowned with St.

Joseph's monastery, keeper of the entrance to the secret caverns where Morgan hid Excalibur.

Dark clouds floated in a bruised sky that grew darker as night quickly conquered day. Sydney trembled with relief. They'd made it.

Bedivere lay on his back beside her, his shield home to a number of arrows meant for them. "The Faraway," he gasped. "We are here."

"Home," Sydney nearly wept as she climbed to her feet, so happy was she to see Glastonbury stretching out below them. She looked around to see if anyone had witnessed their return, but their spot on the Tor was silent and barren. She supposed everyone was at the top, photographing St. Michael's against the sunset backdrop. It was a stunning sight. No one was looking down toward the base of the hill, thank goodness.

Sydney was anxious to get moving, but wondered how they would make it all the way to High Street without attracting attention? She had to see her grandfather. It seemed like forever since she'd been gone, but she knew it had only been days. Even more important than seeing him again, Sydney needed his help. His expertise about King Arthur was essential to finding the Grail. He was the only person who could figure out the mystery behind its hiding place.

The flat was a ten-minute walk from the Tor, down some fairly busy streets. Since neither she nor Bedivere wore 21st century clothing, Sydney was concerned they might attract attention. Then she shook her head with a smile. This was Glastonbury. Half the town paraded around in bizarre clothing on a daily basis, a fact that drove the other half of the town crazy. Anyone who noticed their attire would probably think they worked at the Abbey or were involved in some kind of mystical tour. Worst case, they'd simply assume Sydney and Bedivere were some wacky pilgrims trying to connect with the Goddess.

"C'mon, Bedivere. My grandfather will know what to do. And, you should probably leave that here," Sydney said, nodding at the arrow-studded shield.

Bedivere sheathed Excalibur. He plucked out the arrows, hiding them and the shield in a grove of trees. Soon they were on their way down the sloping hill to where the footpath merged with the street. Bedivere blinked and pulled up short. Sydney could imagine how strange things must seem to him. He'd just traveled thousands of years into the future.

"It's okay. Those are cars. For transportation. They're like wagons, with motors. Just don't step out in front of one while it's moving. They go too fast to dodge properly."

Bedivere nodded and they headed down Chilkwell Street. Thankfully, the raised sidewalk kept them away from the traffic. Sydney urged Bedivere to hurry. If they could get past the intersection at Bere, Chilkwell Street would become more secluded.

No one who crossed their path seemed to pay them much attention. They crossed the street and walked along the Abbey's east wall. Bedivere ran his hand along the earthen stone as if he recognized something that was from a time closer to his own. Sydney smiled. She knew firsthand how it felt to be misplaced in history.

Before long, they veered left and cut along the north wall of the Abbey grounds. Sydney hated to take Silver Street, but it would let them spend the least amount of time on High Street possible. Silver Street was more an alleyway than a street, and she'd been warned from the time she was allowed to wander by herself to avoid it. Sydney never would have taken this route had Bedivere not been at her side. He looked like a body guard, walking with her.

They passed a group of men in tattered clothing huddled together around a trash bin, looking at something they wanted no one else to see. Sydney quickened her step, hoping no one in the group would look up. They didn't.

In moments, they'd reached High Street, then turned the corner onto Magdalene. Her grandfather's bookstore had never looked so good. She led Bedivere through the doorway next to the shop and instantly knew something was wrong.

This hallway shouldn't be silent; her grandfather always played the radio while fixing dinner. Could he be out searching for her? Her stomach knotted at the thought of how worried he must be and she hated that his distress came at her expense. Sydney looked back at Bedivere. His expression was tense, his brows furrowed.

"I have a bad feeling," Sydney whispered. "Something's wrong." As she headed up the staircase, Bedivere grabbed her arm. Drawing Excalibur from the Scabbard, he gently moved her behind him. Excalibur leading the way, they cautiously crept to the second floor. The wooden steps creaked beneath their feet, preventing any stealth. At the top,

Sydney gasped to find door to their flat standing open. Something was definitely wrong.

They stepped inside.

Against the wall to Sydney's right, a couch faced the windows overlooking Magdalene Street. To her left, the tiny kitchen nook was empty. Normally, she would expect to find her grandfather bustling around the kitchen, preparing one of his famous roasts, standing at the sink snapping green beans, or shaving carrots for a stew. Or if dinner was already in the oven, he'd be relaxing in his chair by the window, probably enjoying his pipe and a book.

Instead, Sydney saw him crumpled on the floor near the front window.

"Grandfather!" Sydney cried, racing to his side. She turned him onto his back, searching his face for signs of life. Dropping her head to his chest, she gave him a desperate embrace filled with hope. His heart answered her prayer, beating slow and quiet.

"He's alive, thank God," she sobbed with relief. "But what's happened to him? Bedivere! What are we going to do?"

Bedivere took Sydney's hand in his and dropped to one knee beside her. "We must find the Grail. Its holy magic will return your grandfather to you, just as it will release Arthur from the land of shadows."

Sydney nodded, solemnly. She felt the truth in his words, though she couldn't explain why. Tears silently slipped from her eyes, wetting the shirt of the person she loved most in the world. There was no one to help them, now. She and Bedivere would have to figure out where the Grail was hidden on their own. It was up to them to put things right.

Sydney lay her cheek on her grandfather's chest, and desperately prayed for the strength to make it so.

CHAPTER 12

I looked up from the book. All eyes were on me. I had gotten so lost in the story I'd forgotten where I was, and it was strange to look up and be in the same room I'd just read about. I sat on the ratty couch against the wall. Claire and Doonesbury were at the kitchen table sipping tea. Fern hovered near the windows over the very spot where Sydney and Bedivere found Franklin on the floor.

He perched on the edge of his seat, staring at me. Well, he was still conscious. Fear tugged at my heart. How did this magic work? Was something really going to happen to him now?

We all just sat there, waiting.

Maybe what Claire suspected was true after all. Maybe Sydney Temple hadn't gone into Morgan's Dark Avalon, and there was a different explanation for her disappearance. Maybe this was all just a figment of Fern's hopeful imagination.

As if she felt me thinking about her, Fern turned and smiled at me. Behind her confidence, I could see unease. Even she, the one who'd set this whole thing in motion, the author of this strange adventure, didn't know what was going to happen next.

I opened my mouth to tell her how much I loved Sword Hunters, and that it was a great cliffhanger, but a distant humming through the open window stopped me. It sounded like a helicopter flying close. The humming grew louder, taking on a distinctive pitch, like the buzz of a giant mosquito.

We all exchanged confused looks. Franklin got up from his easy chair and moved to the window and, as he did, the hum became a roar— as if someone had cranked up the volume on a celestial sound system. The walls shook with the decibels.

My head pulsed in pain, the sound slamming into me as a vibration resonated through my entire body. The book slid off my lap and hit the floor. I curled myself into the cushions of the couch, pushing my hands against my ears so hard I thought I might pop my head like a grape.

And then, as suddenly as it had begun, the sound was gone. And in the ringing silence of the hum's wake, I heard a gasp.

I opened my eyes and uncurled myself to find Franklin sprawled on the floor before the window, exactly like the scene from the book. Claire, Doonesbury, and Fern stood over him, triplet expressions of horror on their faces. I felt a shudder ripple through me, raising goose bumps on my arms.

"Oh no!" I breathed.

Doonesbury and Claire dropped to the floor beside him, reflections of Bedivere and Sydney.

"What was that sound?" I quickly joined Claire and Doonesbury on the floor.

"I don't know, do you think that knocked him out?" Claire asked, her voice high with panic.

"Shouldn't we ring emergency or something?" Doonesbury blubbered. "He might have had a heart attack!"

I grabbed my phone from my pocket and punched in 999. "Henderson, wait!" Fern zipped over to me, her expression pained. "We can't call for help. There is only one thing that can help him. You know what that is. You just read the chapter."

I stared at Franklin, then clicked the phone screen off. Claire sat back on her haunches, putting her hands to her cheeks. "I knew something bad was going to happen, I could just feel it!"

Nobody moved or spoke. The silence was eerie.

Silence?

"Hey," I observed, "that hum was so loud it shook the flat. Shouldn't car alarms be going off all over town? Dogs barking? Something?"

We all listened. High Street was as quiet as ever. Maybe even more so. I glanced out the window. A few people strolled along the sidewalks. The cafes were all packed up for the day. Everything seemed fine. A perfectly normal evening.

"Surely we weren't the only ones who heard that hum?"

Doonesbury stared down at Franklin. "Shouldn't we do something? Move him to the couch, at least? It feels wrong just leaving him there lying on the floor."

"He needs to stay there," Fern protested, gently. "That's where Sydney and Bedivere find him. If we weren't here, Franklin would have heard the sound and fallen just as he did, so Sydney could find him."

"So, we're just observers," Doonesbury whispered. "This is so completely bizarre."

The clunk from downstairs made us all freeze. The door to Franklin's flat was still open, and we could hear a girl's voice ring out:

"Grandfather?"

Sydney?

All eyes were glued on the open doorway. Bedivere emerged from the stairwell first, his tall frame draped in a dark tunic of worn leather, Excalibur glowing in his hand. The sword shone with an amazing, surreal light, brighter than the jewels along the hilt and pommel. Bedivere's long, scruffy hair was light brown, the color of cinnamon. Bedivere had the kind of rugged look I would expect from one of King Arthur's knights. He was sweaty and dirty, as if he'd been through a lot to get there, which I knew he had.

Close behind him was a girl about my age who looked amazingly like Tara Benjamin, the girl who played Sydney Wakefield in the movies. But this was Sydney Temple, and she wore a ragged peasant tunic and long skirt. A band of blue cloth tied over her head covered most of her wavy blond hair. Large, fearful eyes stood out in her pale face.

Claire and Doonesbury backed away from Franklin's fallen frame as Sydney pushed past Bedivere and rushed to Franklin's side. "Grandfather!"

Bedivere held Excalibur in a protective way, his eyes demanding obedience as they jumped from me to Claire to Doonesbury. "Who are you? What have you done to this man?" Bedivere demanded.

I expected Doonesbury to say something, after all he was the only other conscious, living adult in the room, but he seemed to be trying to hide behind Claire. Great, we couldn't count on him.

"Don't worry," I ventured, so nervous my voice squeaked. "We didn't hurt him. You're … you're Sir Bedivere."

Bedivere sheathed Excalibur and my heart thumped madly in my chest. One of King Arthur's knights stood in front of me holding the legendary sword Excalibur. It was so amazing that it wasn't even amazing anymore.

"How do you know my name?" Bedivere asked, eyes narrowing.

"We need Fern," Sydney interrupted sharply. She looked up at me, as if seeing me for the first time. "Go find the lady who lives upstairs in the flat right above this one. She'll know what to do."

Fern materialized behind Sydney and met my eyes, a pained expression on her face. Sydney didn't know about Fern. She'd been away so long. This wasn't the right time to tell her, though, she was already upset about her grandfather.

I cut my eyes at Claire and shook my head slightly. I hoped she'd get my meaning. Don't tell her anything yet! "Sorry, Fern isn't home. We tried to ring her before."

Sydney's face scrunched in panicked frustration. "We need some help, someone call 999!" Fern motioned for me to follow her to the kitchenette, and Sydney must have thought I was going to call for help because she turned back to her grandfather, cradling his head in her lap. "Oh, Bedivere," she cried, her eyes filling with tears. "What's happened to him?"

Bedivere dropped to one knee beside her and pulled one of her hands into his. "I cannot say for sure, dear child, but I promise you this. When we find the Grail, its holy magic will return your grandfather to you. Just as it will release Arthur from the land of shadows."

My jaw dropped. The words were exactly what Fern had written. She smiled knowingly, and pointed to the top drawer in a small sideboard. Inside was a bunch of junk, but also a door key on a keychain with a smiling yellow sun on it.

I looked at her and she nodded. "It's the key to my flat. Let's go upstairs." I grabbed it and followed her out the door. In the confusion over Franklin, nobody paid any attention to me.

Fern's flat was much like Franklin's, only nicer. She had a white L-shaped sofa in front of a huge flat-screen television. This room was decorated like someone who had money.

"Okay, now, it wouldn't ordinarily be appropriate to ask a boy your age to look through my nether garments, but clearly we need to get the manuscript. In here now," Fern said with a grin. "And hurry, I don't want Sydney to endure any more than necessary."

I ran to the bedroom. A huge wooden four-poster bed stood against one wall, its white bed spread stark and clean. On the opposite wall by the door was a tall dark dresser with lots of drawers. I dug through the top one, trying to ignore the articles of clothing I touched to uncover the yellow envelope. "Okay, found it. Should I get the typewriter?"

"No time for that now. Go on, quickly," Fern whispered. "Read!"

I slipped the manuscript out of the envelope and read the first few pages. I was shocked. "But, I thought—"

"Henderson," Fern said, interrupting. "Trust me. Now, get back downstairs."

Leaving the beautiful flat behind me, I locked the door and clambered down the staircase in time to hear Sydney cry out, this time in relief.

"Grandfather! Oh, thank goodness, you're all right!"

Franklin pushed himself into a sitting position, with some help from Bedivere. "Sydney! You're here! Thank the stars, you're all right!" He grabbed her up in a hug, squeezing her tight and laughing with utter joy. "It worked, it worked! I knew it would! Yes, I knew it!"

I stood in the doorway watching the scene play out before my eyes, just as it had on the pages I'd just read in Fern's flat—word for word. This was getting really freaky. Fern hovered next to me, a pleased smile on her face. "That's better," she said.

Sydney's head snapped around, hearing Fern's voice for the first time. "Fern? They said you were … " Her words melted away as her eyes focused on Fern's ghostly image. She stood up and slowly approached Fern, spellbound. "What happened to you?"

Bedivere hauled Franklin to his feet, giving him a curious look. Before Bedivere could say anything, Franklin spoke. "Sydney, my dear girl. I know this must be quite a shock."

"Wait, are you …" Sydney asked, her head at a curious tilt. She couldn't say the word.

"I'm afraid so, my dear." Fern's voice was soft and sweet. "It was Modred. He must have wanted desperately to stop you from ruining Morgan's perfect little world. Seems he's been going back and forth through the Doorway for some time now. He and Morgan must know about my books. She must have insisted he find a way to stop the story from being continued. When they couldn't get rid of you, they must have thought that by getting rid of me the story would never reach its end. But with the help of Henderson here, we will complete it."

Sydney's eyes fell on me. The hair on my arms stood up and I felt warmth that spread through my chest and surely showed in my cheeks. I couldn't help it. She was more beautiful than the Sydney I pictured in my head when I'd read the books. Even the dirty, sackcloth dress she wore couldn't make her look bad. She was real, and right in front of me. She met my gaze, really locked eyes on me. My heart flip-flopped and my blood raced. Those eyes were the deepest blue I'd ever seen.

And I fell madly in love with her.

CHAPTER 13

"Do I ... know you?" Sydney whispered.

I swallowed hard, trying to find my voice. "Um, no, we've never met." Except in my dreams, I thought, but I didn't say it. Even in my mind that sounded completely lame.

"You just seem familiar," Sydney said softly. "Hmmm." I moved to the couch and sunk down onto the cushions before my legs gave out. Claire sat beside me as Doonesbury paced the room.

Sydney got up and went to Fern. "I can't believe all this. You're sure it was Modred?"

Fern hadn't talked with me about the details surrounding her death and I was anxious to hear her response. Would she finally explain what exactly had happened?

Franklin interrupted, smoothing his rumpled clothes. "Fern saw Modred in her bedroom the night she died. The Scabbard's magic made him and his mother immortal, but Morgan wouldn't want to be confined to her realm. She gave Dark Avalon a Doorway so that they could come and go, whenever they pleased. Morgan had to keep tabs on the real world in order to control the story. That, I believe," his eyes narrowed sagely, "will be her undoing."

Claire leaned forward, elbows on her knees, deep in thought. "What do you mean, control the story?"

Franklin turned to Bedivere. "Morgan planted the seed for the legend. And Bedivere helped her."

All eyes fell on the knight, who stood protectively behind Sydney, his eyes filled with regret. "I should never have believed her when she promised she would heal him. That one day he would return to rule."

"Not a complete lie, I suppose," Franklin smiled, thinly.

Bedivere swallowed hard, his eyes glazing over with memory. "I saw Arthur best Modred on the battlefield, but that witch healed the traitor. I saw him return, and when she said she would do the same for Arthur … For believing her, I was cursed to watch my King lie helpless and imprisoned in his own kingdom! And I, just as helpless to save him." Tears glimmered in his eyes, swirling with anger that brought him back to the present. "Those two will feel my vengeance someday," he promised.

In the first Sydney Wakefield book, Bedivere tells Sydney the story about the shadow souls of Dark Avalon, how Morgan taunted them, and laughed at their suffering. She had thrown all of Arthur's knights in the dungeons, where they were forced to exist for centuries, in a time limbo. It must have been horrible.

I understood Bedivere's anger.

"Morgan is more powerful than anyone imagined," Franklin said. He rubbed his neck, stretching it like he had a headache, then sunk into his easy chair and picked up his pipe, regarding us. "Morgan's victory wouldn't be as sweet if she had let Arthur die, don't you see? She wanted Arthur to witness Modred ruling in his place for the rest of eternity. All she needed to complete her plan was Excalibur. And that's where Bedivere came in."

Franklin hesitated, his gaze falling again on Bedivere, who hung his head in shame. "Arthur ordered me to throw the sword into the lake," Bedivere moaned. "I didn't want to! Twice I told him it was done. Twice I lied, but he knew. He insisted I return it to the Lady." Bedivere's went to the jeweled hilt of Excalibur at his hip. "If I knew then that she posed as the Lady … how could I know what curse my actions would bring?"

The poor guy seemed really torn up about it. What a drag to have been the one who handed Morgan the power to create Arthur's prison. No wonder he felt so horrible.

Franklin reached out and touched the knight's shoulder. "You couldn't have stopped it. No one could have stopped it." Then he looked at me. "Before now."

Turning to Sydney, he continued. "Do you remember the story about the knight with black armor and red eyes, the one who haunted the Abbey ruins?"

She nodded. "Legend said he was the reason no one really knew what had happened to Arthur, that he kept anyone from uncovering the truth," Sydney said, light dawning in her expression. "Was that Modred?"

"I suspect he's been working to protect Morgan's secret for centuries. At least, centuries in this world." Franklin raised a finger, remembering. "And consider this. The supposed bones of Arthur and Guinevere unearthed by the Abbey monks? If you remember the tale—" He broke off, seeing our blank faces. "In 1189, King Henry II received information regarding the location of Arthur's grave on the Glastonbury Abbey grounds. Supposedly, the tip came from an anonymous Welsh bard."

"Modred again?" asked Claire.

"Highly likely," Franklin settled back into his easy chair, ignoring his pipe this time. "Henry sent the information to the Abbey monks and they dug up the grave. The bones they found were obviously not those of Arthur or Guinevere, since we all know Arthur lies in the glass coffin."

"Who was it in the grave, then?" I asked, leaning forward.

"A blacksmith and his wife. Here's what I believe happened: hundreds of years before that, before the larger Abbey was built, Modred commissioned the smithy to create an iron cross. He requested it be inlaid with Latin script reading: 'Here lies interred in the Isle of Avalon, the renowned King Arthur.' Then Modred killed and buried the poor blacksmith, along with his wife, placing a slab of stone and the iron cross upon them. Then, centuries later, he tipped off King Henry the II.

"After the battle at Camlann, Guinevere had fled to a nunnery in Amesbury, this we know, but stories circulated that after her death, she was buried next to Arthur in secret graves. While Modred certainly spread this rumor as well, he never would have allowed such a thing. He was in love with Guinevere, always had been. It was her final rejection of him that spurred Modred to take over the kingdom while Arthur was away in battle. But when they unearthed the graves on the Abbey grounds, it was certainly in his and his mother's best interest for everyone to think the second body was Guinevere."

"So where was the real Guinevere buried?" Claire asked.

Franklin leaned forward, one of his thick eyebrows raised. "Modred had his final revenge on Guinevere. Posing as a royal official, he met with the Reverend Mother at Amesbury and presented her with what she believed to be a royal decree. It stated that after Guinevere's death her body would be buried in an unmarked grave in the church cemetery—as punishment for her betrayal of Arthur with Lancelot."

Franklin turned his gaze to Fern who hovered beside me. He smiled gently at her. "Modred never forgave Guinevere, but odds are she never forgave herself for betraying Arthur either." In the books, Sydney's grandfather was more than the owner of a bookstore. He was a King Arthur historian, an expert on everything about the legends. The more time I spent with the man the character was based on, the more I realized that was the case in real life as well.

"Well!" Fern said, impatient. "We've certainly determined that Modred spent a great deal of time on our side of the Doorway. He was most definitely here three nights ago."

How did Franklin know all these things about what had happened? Was it because of the dreams of Arthur he and Fern had shared? I was about to ask when Franklin continued.

"Fern, why don't you tell us all what happened that night."

She moved to the other side of the room, then back again as she spoke. "That evening I walked up the Tor. I liked to go there at sunset." Fern looked at Sydney, her eyes soft. "I stayed long after the sun went down. I walked back, stopped by Pilgrim's Inn for a late dinner and a pint. When I got home, I found him sitting in the dark, at my kitchen table. Black cloak and all. I knew it was Modred immediately."

With a shiver, I remembered the black-cloaked man I'd seen outside. Could it have been Modred?

Fern went on, her eyes closed, lost in the memory. I dared not interrupt. "I knew I was in trouble. I tried to get to the telephone, but the room started filling up with this white smoke, some alchemy of Morgan's, I suppose. It smelled foul, like burning tallow. Sweaty and earthy and musty. I was terrified. My whole body went numb, and that's the last thing I remember about being alive."

We all sat in silence, Franklin nodding as if he recognized the concoction used as a murder weapon. My stomach clenched. What had made me think I wanted to hear about Fern's last living moments? It was totally depressing. Yet even now, she was such a life force that she filled the room with warmth. Ugly hatred for Modred swirled through me like poison, infecting every thought. I wanted to do whatever it took to destroy both him and his witch of a mother. If that was him outside, watching Fern's flat … the thought made my stomach hurt even worse. I pulled out my lucky rock and rubbed my thumb against the rough surface. I was about to tell everyone what I'd seen when Fern zipped over to me.

"What is that?" she asked, staring at the rock, her eyes wide and round.

I held it up between my thumb and forefinger so she could see. "It's just my lucky rock."

"Where did you get it?" Fern's fingers touched the rock hanging from the leather strap around her neck.

"Bedivere? What's wrong?"

The knight stumbled backward, white as a sheet, his skin slick with sweat. He sank onto the couch next to Claire, shivering violently. Sydney grabbed a blanket off the back of the couch and wrapped it around him. Bedivere pulled his knees up and lay on his side.

"It's happening," I breathed, looking at Fern as I stuck the rock back into my pocket.

"What's happening?" Sydney asked, her voice wet with fear. She looked at Fern, searching for an answer. Fern's eyes hadn't left my face. She nodded, giving permission for me to answer the question.

"I have Fern's manuscript for Into the Faraway right here," I said, nervously. "I just read the first section—Franklin woke up, which happened. But Bedivere also got sick."

"What do you mean, sick?" Sydney blurted, turning on Fern, in shock. "Why would you write such a thing?"

Fern's expression was stoic. "Sydney, Bedivere is not of this world. The part of him that existed on this plane died fifteen hundred years ago. This shadow that Morgan captured was not meant to exist anywhere but Dark Avalon. If he stays here, he won't survive. He can't."

Sydney burst into tears. "Why didn't you bring him back with me then?" She turned to Franklin, pleading. "We have to take him back! Please, he can't die! He's done nothing but help me! All he wants is to free Arthur. Please!"

"Yes, he needs to get back to Avalon as soon as possible," Franklin agreed. "But we can't do that without the item you returned to our world to find."

Chapter 14

We were off to find the Holy Grail.

Yep. *The* Holy Grail.

No big deal. Only the most sought-after relic in human history. And we were just going to head on out and find it.

Franklin filled a knapsack with plastic water bottles while he explained that although Sydney thought she'd only been gone for a week or so, she'd actually been gone three years. That news shook her up a bit, but she recovered quickly. She was amazing, actually. Finding out I'd lost three years of my life would have seriously freaked me out. But I guess Sydney had more important things on her mind. Like saving Bedivere.

Claire volunteered to stay behind and watch over the knight. Doonesbury said he'd drive the Renault. Franklin, with Excalibur strapped around his skinny hips, rode shotgun. Sydney and I, manuscript tucked securely in my backpack, took the back seat. I'd looked for the cloaked figure as we raced out of the flat, but I couldn't see anyone hovering around that spire. 'Course, it was pretty dark.

Time was of the essence for Bedivere and we needed to high-tail it over to Chalice Gardens. Franklin said that's where we would find the Grail. Doonesbury turned the key and fired up the Renault's engine.

"Uh, Franklin?" I asked, my voice high and nervous. "Haven't people been searching for the Grail for, oh, I don't know … forever? How do you know it's in Chalice Gardens?"

Sydney piped up. "Fortuna did tell us the Grail was hidden near a magical well." Fortuna, the elf who helped them find Excalibur in the tunnels beneath the Tor, had told her this in the last book, Sword Hunters. "Chalice Well actually makes sense. Fortuna did say its hiding place would not be revealed until the Grail was needed for a holy purpose," Sydney continued.

"The quest for the Holy Grail was Arthur's venture into folly," Franklin growled. "He is a great man and a great king, but he is still just a man, subject to the desires and ridiculous notions of any man. Turn left there," he directed Doonesbury, pointing out a side street. "Arthur and the Knights saw many visions of the Grail, but the real cup always eluded them. Arthur wanted it, but he never needed it. A holy purpose, Fortuna said. Yes, indeed. Now, it is ready to be found."

"This is all so strange," I murmured, and beside me on the back seat, Sydney nodded in agreement.

"Tell me about it," Sydney sighed. "I haven't felt like myself in days! It's like I've stepped into someone else's skin, like I'm living their life. I can't believe I've actually been gone so long ..." Her voice trailed off.

I nodded. "So, what was it like when you went through the Doorway that first time? Did you realize right away what had happened?"

Sydney thought for a moment. "It took a while for everything to sink in. At first, I didn't realize I was actually in the story. But the more that things happened the way they'd happened in the book," she paused and swallowed hard, "well, it was terrifying."

"Yeah, I read it."

"Right. Fern said you reading her books was the magic that made it happen? Something to do with you and her old flat in London?" She shook her head like the whole thing was too much.

I swallowed. "I feel like I should apologize."

"Don't be ridiculous. You saved me! I'd still be stuck in story limbo." Sydney grabbed my hand and squeezed it. I felt my face turn red again and I was glad for the darkness of the car. It actually hurt me when she let go.

Sydney went on. "I really started freaking out as we neared what I knew was the end of Doorway to Avalon. I mean, I'd read it. When I knew what was about to happen, I could plan for it. I knew there was a cliffhanger. I had no idea what would happen next. I kept hoping Fern was writing me home."

"And so she did," I smiled.

Sydney looked at me and smiled back. "Yeah."

I could barely breath. I couldn't believe I was talking to Sydney Wakefield. Okay, Sydney Temple, but really, it was the same thing.

"So, are you and Claire in Fern's books, too?" she asked.

"Oh! No, we're not. Neither is Doonesbury. The pages I read are just you and Franklin going to Chalice Well."

"Oh, right, that makes sense," Sydney nodded.

"I'm just a reader here. Not even a supporting character."

"I don't know about that," she smiled again, and my face flushed hotter.

They pulled into a car park and screeched to a halt. "Let's go," Franklin announced. "Margaret will meet us here." He had telephoned somebody before we left the flat, making arrangements for us to be let into the Gardens. He said one of the caretakers was a friend.

Sydney seemed to know her too. "Are you sure we won't get Margaret into trouble for this, Grandfather?"

"Don't worry, my dear," he answered, holding the door open for us to get out. "Margaret is quite aware of what's at stake here. She's thrilled to be part of it."

At one end of the car park, a wooden door displayed a hand-painted, emerald EXIT sign. As we approached, the door silently swung open revealing a woman in a long, patchwork dress. Her hair was long and braided into a thick black plait that hung over her shoulder like a big dark snake.

"Quietly, please," she whispered with just a trace of an English accent. "Hugh's asleep in front of the telly and I'd like to keep him there."

"You're an angel, Margaret," Franklin said, kissing her cheek as he passed. "This is history in the making, my dear."

"But you'll be history if Hugh catches you out here," Margaret warned him. "Promise you'll respect the Gardens?"

"You have my solemn word, good lady. You'll never know we were here," Franklin said, bowing deeply. Margaret didn't notice her friend wore a Sword said to exist only in storybooks.

"I'll go keep an eye on Hugh. Play defense if he wakes up." Margaret winked as we passed through the door.

"Let's move quickly. We haven't much time," Franklin instructed as we left her behind. Sydney snapped on a flashlight, shining the beam along the cobbled walk before us. I heard the fountain before I saw it to our right. It glowed, reflecting the pale moonlight—a waterfall made up of a series of smooth bowl-shaped stones. The water dribbled down the stones into a shallow, circular pool. Intersecting this first pool was another circular pool, like two rings intertwined, creating a figure eight.

I searched the misty darkness, seeing walled gardens heavy with growth. Brilliant leaves of luminescent orange and red were visible in the half-light. I imagined it was beautiful here in sunlight.

The temperature had dropped considerably and a cold wind pushed at our backs. The path veered right, leading to an opening in one of the vine-covered walls. We followed Franklin through the opening as he explained. "This is the section of the Gardens called 'King Arthur's Court.' Over here is the Pilgrim's Bath, or healing pool. This area was a popular attraction 150 years ago before modern medicine began performing more miracles than these waters. More importantly to us, this particular place in the Gardens is where the ley lines of Michael and Mary converge." He stopped, turning to face us. "Do you understand about ley lines?"

Sydney explained. "They have to do with the alignment of various geographical places. Like, on a map you can draw a straight line from Stonehenge to the Tor, another between the Tor and the site of the Cadbury hill fort, and another back to Stonehenge to create a triangle."

"Thousands of significant points on the globe are connected," Franklin added. "Many of these ley lines are named. Michael and Mary intersect right in King Arthur's Court, which makes it an extremely significant point, at least as far as we are concerned."

Franklin stopped in the middle of a courtyard. To our right was a rectangular-shaped pool fed by another waterfall that poured out of the wall in front of us. Water splashed over a series of squared-off rocks.

"Why does that water look so dark?" I asked, moving closer to it.

"In the daylight it actually looks red," Franklin answered. "Some say it is Christ's blood, but there is a high iron content in the water. However, it is an interesting coincidence, given what's hidden nearby."

Franklin reached his right hand across his body and took hold of Excalibur. "Stand back!" he commanded.

We did as we were told, as Franklin unsheathed the Sword. It glowed as if lit from within. It wasn't just reflecting moonlight. This was a magical Sword.

Franklin swiveled Excalibur in his hand, handing the hilt to Sydney. "You do the honors. After all, this is your quest."

Stepping aside, he motioned to a stone bench that jutted out to the right of the waterfall. Sydney looked lost. "I'm not sure what you mean for me to do with this."

Franklin paused. "Right. Look just there, beneath the seat."

We all dropped down to our haunches, peering under the bench. Doonesbury directed the beam of the flashlight so we could see. He shrugged. "I don't see anything at all. Just a bench."

Franklin squatted beside us. "It should be right there!" He felt around under the stone, his brow furrowed. Then he turned to me. "Henderson, the manuscript!"

Of course! I had to read the words before whatever was going to happen to the bench would ... happen.

"This is sure going to slow things down," I grumbled, fumbling in the backpack for the envelope. Doonesbury handed me the flashlight. I skipped quickly over the paragraphs I'd already read, skimming until I found the right passage.

"Here. Sydney and Franklin Temple are in the Garden, right where we are." I read quickly, but I tried not to skim. "There should be a slot just beneath the seat. Slide Excalibur into it and turn the Sword."

I turned the flashlight beam back at the bench. Sydney squinted. "Yes, I see it now! A slot between the stones!"

"Fascinating," Franklin muttered.

Doonesbury looked again. "I swear that wasn't there before."

Sydney held Excalibur in both hands and slid the length of the blade into the slot. It fit perfectly. The hilt clunked against the stone.

"Okay, now what?" asked Sydney, keeping a tight hold on the sword.

"Do as Henderson says. Give it a turn," Franklin said, excitement in his voice. My heart raced. It was another surreal moment, unbelievably thrilling but mostly just unbelievable. If this actually worked, we were about to see the most holy relic of all time. The most important cup ever. The Holy Grail.

Sydney wiggled the handle of the sword, testing out which direction it would turn most easily. It clicked to the left, like a key unlocking a door. A startled "oh!" popped from her lips and she fell backward away from the bench, which was a good thing because a burst of old, dusty air blew out as the seat of the bench began to rise up.

"Good God," Doonesbury breathed, as spellbound as the rest of us.

"Jeez, Henderson, you could have warned me," Sydney said, climbing to her feet and wiping the dirt off her hands.

"Sorry," I said, a hot flush of shame running up my neck again.

Franklin removed Excalibur from the "lock" and slid it back into the Scabbard. "Finish the chapter now Henderson, if you please," he asked.

I read quickly again, the light from the flashlight dimming as if the batteries weakened. When I looked up, Franklin motioned toward the opening with his arm. "Don't tell us anything about what you read, Master Green," he warned. "Let's go."

"I'm having trouble reading these last few lines," I said. Doonesbury shook the flashlight as Sydney peered through the opening.

"There's a ladder here," she told us. "C'mon!"

"But I haven't—" I began, as Doonesbury pushed the flashlight into my hands and followed her and Franklin down the ladder. I shook it, and tried to take in the final paragraph of the chapter.

"Are you coming?" Sydney called.

"Right, yes!" The flashlight had a hook attached to its strap, so I snapped it onto the belt loop of my pants and climbed in. At the bottom of the ladder, I realized we were in a narrow tunnel that led into darkness. I aimed the flashlight into its depths, dimly illuminating a red door at the end. Sydney reached the door first, lifting the ancient handle to reveal a chamber as breathtaking and bright as Fern had described it. The illumination came from the thing the chamber was created to hold.

No one spoke, as if putting eyes on the Grail stole our ability to create sound.

Franklin was the first to find his voice. "There it is," he whispered, reverently. "That which so many have sought, yet none could ever find. Now this magnificent Chalice will help us usher in a new era." Franklin looked at us as if we were his students and he was lecturing about a historical event. "The world will never be the same after this, my friends. I've waited a long, long time for this day … "

He pulled a folded cloth from his back pocket and shook it loose of its folds; a scrap of old tie-dyed t-shirt. The Cup wasn't gold or silver or anything like you might expect a cup this important to be. It was a stone goblet, dark brown and rugged, looking like something a kindergartener would make. It had a wide base that tapered up into the rounded cup part, separated by a molded line darker than the rest. The Cup hung in mid-air surrounded by an unearthly glow, like a star twinkling in the sky. It looked like Christmas.

Franklin reached out and plucked the Cup from the air. The glow continued to fill the room until the cloth was wrapped around it. The cloth seemed to extinguish the light as it wrapped around the Cup, holding it in until it was needed. Somehow, I knew that when the cloth was removed, light would spill everywhere. I could tell that this wasn't the kind of light that could ever go out permanently.

Franklin tucked the wrapped cup into my pack along with the manuscript, leaving us in only the flickering light of the flashlight.

"Amazing," Doonesbury said, in an airy, peaceful voice.

"Yes, but we can't stand here gaping over a miracle," Sydney barked, all business. "We've got to get back to Bedivere."

"Right," Franklin agreed, removing two plastic liter-bottles from my pack. "But the Chalice is only part of the equation. We must gather water from the Lion's Head."

After we climbed back up the ladder, Franklin placed Excalibur in the keyhole slot, turning it to the right. The lid slowly closed until it fell back into place with a deep thunk as the sound of solitary, sarcastic applause broke the darkness.

A tall man leaned against the doorway of the small courtyard. He wore a dark cloak, the hood pushed back to reveal dark, angry eyes. "Well, well. The blasted thing actually does exist. I must say, old man, I never believed it."

"Modred," Franklin snarled.

"Oh no," breathed Sydney.

"Oh yes, child. It is I." He pulled back one side of his cloak to reveal a sword, the handle of which he fingered menacingly. "I have come for the Grail."

Chapter 15

"Surely you don't think we've actually found the Grail?" Excalibur in hand, Franklin stepped forward, moving in front of me. "That's just stuff of legends."

Modred strode quickly through the thick mist of the courtyard. "Don't toy with me," he snarled. "Why else would you be in Chalice Gardens in the dead of night if not to retrieve the third element for your precious granddaughter?"

Even in the blue moonlight, Modred's dark eyes gleamed. He was definitely the same black-cloaked guy I'd seen following us around. Seeing him closer I could tell something was wrong with his skin. His face was covered with lines and bumps.

"I see time waits for no man," Franklin appraised Modred's face, eyebrow arched. A sinister growl rose in Modred's throat. Franklin lifted Excalibur in warning. "I wouldn't try anything if I were you. We've one more stop to make, and then we're leaving this place. Even if we have to go through you to do it."

Modred swirled his cape up over his left shoulder and drew his own sword with a metallic *schwing*! "You're not going anywhere until you give me what I came for. And perhaps ... not even then."

"Is this what you want?" Franklin chided, indicating the Scabbard strapped to his hip. "From appearances, I'd say you most definitely need it."

I realized what Franklin meant. When the Scabbard was taken out of Dark Avalon, its magic went with it. Now, Modred and his mother were aging. No wonder he seemed so desperate. His entire existence was slipping away.

"Surrender the elements or die," said Modred. Franklin put his arm out to move us away from him. We were only too happy to move closer to the stone bench.

This wasn't exactly a large area for a sword fight. I couldn't imagine how an ancient man like Franklin Temple could overpower someone like Modred, no matter what kind of powers Excalibur held. I didn't know how we'd get out of there with the Grail, much less back to the flat alive. Of course, if we didn't get back to the flat with the Grail, Bedivere was done for.

My heart pounded. I tried to think of some way to distract Modred, to give Franklin the advantage. But someone was ahead of me.

Near the healing pool off to our left, a shimmering glow appeared in the mist. The glow materialized into Fern and, from where we huddled behind Franklin, I could tell that Modred had seen her too.

"Trapped between worlds, hmmm? What a perfect place for you."

"If you thought killing me would stop the story," said Fern, triumphant, "you were wrong. Your selfish, evil ways will lead to tragedy!"

Modred hesitated as if her words meant something to him. Then he started to laugh. He cackled, loud and sarcastic. The sound echoed off the courtyard's stone walls.

"Why were you following me?" I yelled, without even thinking first. "After you killed Fern, why didn't you just go back to Avalon and stay there?"

Modred regarded me coolly, tilting his head to the side in appraisal.

Sydney grabbed my arm in warning. "Henderson, don't."

Modred glared at Sydney, his eyes sparking with hatred. "Don't what, my dear? Don't talk to the awful man who killed your beloved Fern? Don't you want to know how I discovered the woman had deceived me, once again?" He turned his glare back to Fern. "Once you were dead, I thought it was over. Finally, blessedly, over. But I had other business to tend to before my return through the Doorway, the last being a stop at the office of Stanley Doonesbury."

Every head whipped toward Stanley, our expressions shocked and accusatory. He shook his head emphatically. "I've never seen this man before in my life!"

"I needed to know what would happen to the stories once Fern was gone," said Modred with an evil smile. "The girl told me. A ghost writer. I had to ask her what that meant, but oh, it is so ironic."

He turned to me. "And then she told me about a young boy who insisted Fern Caldwell's ghost had appeared to him. And that the ghost wanted him to help her finish writing the story. I knew right away what had to be done." None of us had moved a muscle.

"That is a lovely flat in Sloane Gardens. I settled down to wait for cover of darkness. I saw your Mother come home. Beautiful thing, she is. And then you and your sister left … " He looked around, as if realizing for the first time that not all of us were present. "I decided to follow you. I hope your neighbor will not miss his car too much."

"You know how to drive?" Doonesbury said, then seemed to wish he hadn't.

Modred glared at him "Enough chit-chat," he said, brandishing his sword again. "Are we going to do this the easy way? Please say we're not. I've been so looking forward to the hard way." He was quick, lunging past me to grab Sydney before any of us realized he was even moving. I rushed at them, not knowing where all this bravery was coming from. I mean the man had a sword. Seriously.

Sydney twisted and squirmed, hitting at him with her fists. With me in the mix, Modred had to shove at us both. Sydney tumbled to the ground. I tripped backwards, as Modred raised his sword, looming over Sydney.

The next second, I'd thrown myself between them. "NO!"

"NO!" Someone else yelled the exact same word at the exact same moment. Then a flash of bright white light knocked Modred off his feet, propelling him hard into the courtyard wall. He thumped to the ground, the sword clanging to the cobblestones.

I helped Sydney up. "Are you okay?"

"I'm fine," she said, rubbing her elbow. "What was that flash?" she asked, brushing dirt and leaves from her tunic.

"Franklin," Doonesbury stammered, pointing at the old man. "Franklin happened."

Sydney and I turned to look at her grandfather. He had a ghostly aura around him, crackles of electricity sparking around his hands.

That magical bolt of energy had come from Franklin Temple.

CHAPTER 16

"You have ... *magic?*" I heard Fern shout, as she floated past us toward Franklin. "But how? How could you, I mean, who are you?"

Franklin quickly sheathed Excalibur, acting as if nothing had happened. "No time to explain now. We must return to Bedivere. Let's go, quickly." He snatched up the bottles and headed up the short, stone staircase that stood to the left of the waterfall. At the top, he paused. "Doonesbury, grab Modred's sword. Everyone! Hurry! This way to the Lion's Head."

Doonesbury moved tentatively to Modred's fallen body, easing himself toward the sword as if Modred might sit up and snatch it. But nothing like that happened. Modred was out cold. Or dead. I just hoped he'd stay that way long enough for us to get back to the flat.

Stanley lifted the sword from the ground. It was nearly half his length. Grabbing the hilt in both hands, he dragged the heavy sword toward the steps. The blade sparked and scraped against the stone path.

"Can you manage it?" Franklin asked, hovering at the top of the steps, wisps of a strange aura continuing to swirl around him, mixing with the misty night.

"Of course, I can—"

Franklin sighed and returned to the courtyard, grabbing the sword from Doonesbury's hands. Franklin carried it as if it weighed no more than a feather. Doonesbury's eyes grew even wider.

"Have I completely gone mad?" he whispered, echoing my own thoughts. It was as if Franklin Temple had been taken over by some magical superhero. We all followed him to the next section of the garden in stunned silence.

"Grandfather?" Sydney began. She didn't seem to know what to make of all this any more than we did.

"Later, Sydney," he said, putting one hand on her shoulder. "I promise."

She conceded with a nod and followed him back up the stairs. At the top, a gravel path cut through a grassy lawn to a half-moon shaped pool. The spring flowed through this section to the waterfall below, making its way from the actual Chalice Well higher up on the hill. At this secondary point, the water flowed from the mouth of a stone lion's head that looked like someone's doorknocker. The figure protruded from a thigh-high wall covered with foliage. Franklin explained this was the spot where the multitudes of people who came to this place for its healing properties drank the waters.

"You can drink this water?" I asked. "But isn't it old?"

"The well is ancient, but the water has flowed from this spring since man first walked this ground. It has never run dry, not even in the fiercest drought. The spring has often been the saving grace of this community. Many claim its waters have healed them of disease. They say it's magical. Blessed. Holy."

"You seem to be pretty magical yourself," Doonesbury asked pointedly as Franklin filled the bottles.

"You will see for yourself in a few minutes just what this water can do. We'll discuss the rest later. Now is not the time. To the car!"

We backtracked down the steps to the courtyard, horrified to find it empty.

"Where did he go?" said Sydney, looking around as if expecting an ambush.

Fern materialized in the spot where Modred was lying when we left the courtyard. "He ran away like the coward he is. But he'll be waiting for us. Now that he's sure we have everything we need to save Arthur, he'll be ready." She glared at Franklin, who acted like he didn't see her.

"No time to worry about Modred now, we must get back to Bedivere. Hurry!" Franklin rushed us through the garden and out the EXIT gate where we piled back into the Renault.

As Doonesbury sped back to the flat, I felt Sydney looking at me. "What?" I asked.

"You saved my life. Again."

My heart raced. "Me? Franklin did, whatever … he did."

"Well, yes, but you put yourself between me and Modred. That was so brave."

Brave wasn't a word usually used about me.

Sydney smiled and reached over to squeeze my hand. Then her expression shifted. "Did you know about Franklin? Was that in the pages you read?"

The jolt shook me. I hadn't even thought about that. "No! I stopped at the part where they opened the way into the Grail."

The car was silent for a moment. "Let me see the manuscript," Sydney said, reaching for my backpack. She pulled out the pages and reached up to switch on the overhead light. "I was on page twenty-four," I explained. She flipped through the pages and when she reached page twenty-five, my heart stopped beating.

It was blank.

"Uh-oh," Sydney and I said, simultaneously.

"What is it?" Franklin asked from the front seat.

"Henderson only read to the end of that last chapter, where we find the Grail. After that, the pages are blank!" Sydney cried. "Does that mean we can't save Bedivere?" She was panic-stricken.

"Calm down, my dear, all will be well. We're here. Nothing has stopped us from arriving." There was a parking spot on the street across from the Town Hall, and Doonesbury steered to the curb. Before he was properly parked, we'd scrambled out of the car. Sydney was the first one up the stairs, anxious to make sure Bedivere was still with us.

I followed close behind, shocked to find Claire on her knees next to the couch, her face in her hands, weeping.

"There was nothing I could do!" she cried, reaching out to Sydney, desperate to explain. "He just kept growing older and older!"

We gathered around the couch, gaping at what was left of Sir Bedivere. His skin was withered and old, his skin grey, his hair completely silver. Time was catching up with him.

"Quick, the Grail!" Franklin unscrewed the top of one of the bottles while Sydney yanked the pack of my back and dug through it, sobbing all the while. The scrap of tie-dyed shirt fell away, and that same amazing light poured into the room, like day dawned early.

Claire's breath caught and her tears stopped immediately. Her expression melted into rapture. The light from the Grail affected

Bedivere as well. In its glow, his skin seemed softer, less grey, his face and hands not quite as bony.

"Quick!" Franklin urged, pouring some of the water we'd collected at the well into the Chalice. "Pour it in his mouth, hurry!"

Sydney held the back of Bedivere's head with one hand and brought the Cup to his lips with the other. "Drink," she whispered.

At first, the water just poured into his mouth and out over his chin, but then, suddenly, he gulped. He closed his mouth around the lip of the Cup and drank with gusto.

"Yes! It's working!" Sydney cried, sobbing with relief.

"Whooooooo! Brilliant!" I crowed in triumph, throwing one fist in the air and pumping it.

Color flowed back into Bedivere's cheeks. His hair changed back into its original color, and the lines on his face and hands melted away.

Stunned, Claire moved toward me like a zombie. I gave her a huge hug. "It's okay, Claire. Everything's going to be okay." She laid her head on my shoulder, and I could feel her tears on my neck.

"Oh, HG, it was so awful. He was dying and I couldn't do anything to save him."

"It's over now." I patted her back and remembered the times when I was younger and she'd comforted me. Funny how things could change. "Our brave knight is going to be just fine, see?"

Claire pulled away from me and looked at Bedivere, who sat up on the couch, looking better than even when he and Sydney first arrived. "He is, isn't he?" Claire said through a hitched sob. "It's a miracle, that's what it is. A miracle! I've never seen one before but that's what this is."

I could tell Claire's head was spinning, so I helped her to Franklin's easy chair. "Just take it easy, sis. You gotta breathe, okay? Because there's more amazing stuff to come."

"Like the story of our Franklin Temple, for instance." I turned to find Fern standing next to me. "I imagine that will be quite an amazing story." She glared at him.

My eyes darted to Franklin, who took the tie-dyed cloth and wrapped up the Grail again. With a sigh, he returned it to my pack, then unbuckled Excalibur. He put it and its Scabbard on the floor next to Bedivere. No one in the room spoke. Franklin reached out to Fern, as if it was possible to take her hands.

"Don't." Fern floated backwards, out of his reach. "I just want to know what's going on, and I want to know right now."

"Of course you do." Franklin looked hurt.

Claire leaned closer to me. "Why is Fern so angry?" she whispered.

I tried to explain. "Modred ambushed us at Chalice Gardens. He would have killed us all if it weren't for Franklin." I figured I'd try to spin things in the old guy's favor. I wasn't exactly sure why Fern was so angry. Stranger things had certainly happened to me in the last week than finding out a friend had magical powers. "He cast some kind of spell, a big flash of light that knocked Modred onto his butt!" I grinned at Franklin. "It was wicked cool."

Franklin acknowledged my admiration with a slight nod.

Claire shook her head. "Too much stuff to compute. I swear my brain is shutting down."

"I don't blame you, my dear," Franklin said, gently. "But I think I know why our friend Fern is upset with me."

"Oh, you do, do you?" Fern snipped, folding her arms over her chest.

"I lied to you. And I'm sorry."

"Really? You lied? I hadn't guessed that yet." Her sarcasm was biting and cold. "You have magic and you thought it was better to keep such a thing from me? Your best friend?"

Franklin dropped his eyes. "I'm sorry, but I'm afraid it's more than the magic. There are so many things I haven't told you—things I haven't been able to tell you all these years. So often I've wished I could and now I will. I'll tell you everything." He turned to Sydney. "You as well, Sydney. You deserve to know the truth. And now that everyone is healthy enough to hear," he smiled at Bedivere, "I suppose I should start with my name." He paused. "It is not Franklin Temple."

Sydney put a hand to her mouth. The rest of us exchanged uneasy looks. "What do you mean?" Sydney breathed. "Then, who are you?"

Franklin arched a grey eyebrow and shrugged.

"I used to be called Merlin."

Chapter 17

"No. Way," I gawked.

"I knew it," Bedivere breathed, a huge smile on his face.

I'd been hanging out with Merlin? The Merlin?

"What?" Fern gasped.

"But, I don't understand. How can that be?" Sydney stammered, backing away from her grandfather/Merlin, a.k.a. the GREATEST WIZARD OF ALL TIME. "But, you're my grandfather! How could my grandfather be someone who lived all those years ago? That's impossible!" Sydney was right, that would make Franklin a pretty old guy. We all looked at him for an answer. Everyone but Fern, who apparently thought she knew.

"Magic," Fern seethed. "It all makes perfect sense. Morgan was his student. If she was powerful enough to figure out a way to cheat death, do you think the great Merlin couldn't?"

"I'm sorry you're so angry, Fern," Franklin/Merlin said, shaking his head. "But that same magic has always been here to help you; to protect you."

"A lot of help and protection it was the night Modred showed up in my flat! And don't you think that given the subject of my life's work I just might have wanted to know that my best friend and confidant was the subject matter's closest ally?" A glowing, deep red mist materialized around Fern, making it look like someone was shining a red spotlight on her. It was creepy and the old wizard didn't seem to like it much either.

"Fern, please, calm down. I couldn't tell you; surely you must understand that. It was important that you not depend on me for the answers you were meant to discover yourself."

Fern faded to a dark orange, then to sort of a yellow. This seemed to be a good thing, like maybe she was considering what he'd said. "I do not like being lied to."

Franklin/Merlin dropped his eyes. "I understand completely. But truly, if there's anyone in this room who deserves to be angry with me, it isn't you." He looked at his granddaughter. "It's Sydney."

Sydney frowned. "Why do you say that? So you figured out a way to live for fifteen hundred or so years." She shook her head. "I guess at some point in the last century you got married, had children … "

"No, Sydney." Merlin shook his head, his face sad with truth. He moved to the window and looked out.

"But … that's what you told me!" The volume of her voice grew with each word. "My mother died in childbirth and daddy was killed in a motorcycle accident. That's what you said!"

"I'm so sorry, Sydney." He didn't turn around.

"You can't do this!" Tears pooled in her eyes. "My whole life has been a lie, is that what you're saying?"

"I know it must seem that way at the moment and I understand you would have liked me to be more honest with you, but you must trust me when I say it was for your protection."

For an all-powerful wizard, Merlin certainly wasn't working any magic at the moment. He sighed and ran his hands over his cheeks as he pondered his words, finally turning back to her. "There are many emotions tumbling around inside me at the moment," he began, "but while a great deal of regret is amongst them, there is also an immense amount of love."

He met Sydney's gaze, raising his eyebrows for emphasis. "Regardless of who your natural parents may be, you are my child. I raised you from infancy. I cared for you when you were sick. I bathed you. I clothed you. I counseled you when you were sad or worried. All those things I did because I love you." His eyes grew misty. "I and I alone was chosen to be that person to you. That was a gift for which I shall forever be thankful."

Sinking into his chair, he sighed. "If you will sit and listen, without interruption, I will tell you the entire story. I must be quick however, because the hour grows ever later and we have other important things to discuss."

We all agreed. Even Fern was silent, anxious to hear what he had to say. Claire sunk to the floor next to the couch. I joined her and Sydney sat beside me. I briefly worried about getting home before Mom woke up, we still had a long drive ahead of us, but no way was I missing this. Hopefully, Mom would sleep until morning.

Merlin cracked open the window next to his easy chair and the chilly night air slipped into the room. With the flick of a finger, a roaring fire appeared in the fireplace next to him. We all jumped at the unexpected magic, but were thankful as its warmth curled around us like a comfortable blanket. Merlin lit his pipe, took a big pull, and let the smoke drift out the window.

"For you to understand how Sydney came to be my granddaughter, I have to first explain how I failed Arthur." This seemed to be difficult for him to say and he cleared his throat a couple of times before he went on.

"I was the King's advisor. His protector. I had warned Arthur for years that one day Modred would betray him. I never knew how or when, but I knew it would happen." Merlin sighed. "Such is the mystery of magic. It is not a perfect science.

"For example, I didn't know the meeting between Arthur and Modred at Camlann was pre-arranged by Morgan so she could get her hands on Excalibur. I didn't suspect she was trying to steal the Sword to create her own version of Avalon, to make Arthur her prisoner.

"At that point, Morgan had already stolen the Scabbard. Its magic had saved Arthur's life more times than I could count, and without its protection, he could be killed. Morgan knew if Arthur was close to death, he would return Excalibur to the Lake, as he'd promised the day he received the Sword.

"Morgan was the new Lady of the Lake—the spiritual leader of the real Avalon. The former Lady was her sister Vivienne. They were both my students. But Vivienne had given it over to her, after falling in love with me."

Claire gave a little gasp. I swallowed hard. I could hear the emotion in Merlin's voice as his expression saddened. "Vivienne knew that as long as she was Lady of the Lake, we could never be together. Morgan knew this too, and so she convinced Vivienne that by stepping down, she and I would be free to marry. Morgan arranged a secret meeting for the two of us."

He paused, took a deep breath, then went on. "It was a trap of course. Morgan placed a powerful spell on two ancient oak trees, capturing Vivienne inside one, me in the other. We stood next to each other for centuries, unable to move or speak. Today, those trees are called Gog and Magog. They stand just on the other side of the Tor from here. My tree was the one you used to escape from the tunnels beneath the Tor, Sydney."

Sydney seemed as mesmerized by the story as were we all. "It took me years to free myself, and when I did, the tree remained. My escape here caused a rupture in the shadow realm, and a chasm that connected my tree to the tunnels."

"But what happened to Vivienne?" Doonesbury asked, his voice tense with anticipation. "Did you free her, too?"

Merlin raised his eyes, wet with emotion. "She remains trapped in that tree, even now. After all this time, I have never found a way to release her. It confounds me because the combination of my magic and hers certainly should have been enough. Perhaps Vivienne was so incapacitated by Morgan's betrayal that she didn't want to escape, I don't know. I believe it will take Morgan's death to release her." He cleared his throat again.

I raised my hand as if we were in school, but quickly dropped it. "Uh, how did you find out everything that had happened while you were trapped in the tree? You said you knew Morgan had set a trap for you. But how did you know what she had done after the battle? About Dark Avalon?"

Franklin closed his eyes, gathering his thoughts. "I knew Morgan had betrayed Vivienne and I, and I'd heard the stories like everyone else: Morgan had taken Arthur away to heal him. I knew that couldn't be true. But everyone was gone by then, all I had were the legends. Then, one day I saw Modred. The legends told of Arthur killing him on the battlefield, but there he was. I followed him, and watched him summon the Doorway and disappear through it.

"Many times after that I tried to go through the Doorway myself, but I could never make the magic work. Then, one stormy winter night, I had a dream. The kind I often had foretelling the future."

I couldn't help the shiver.

"In my dream, I saw Arthur in his glass coffin prison. I saw him in Morgan's Dark Avalon. I felt so helpless—how could I save him if I couldn't reach him? And then, the dream shifted. I saw an infant, and I knew, beyond a shadow of a doubt that this child would someday save Arthur. I saw this child wrapped in a many-colored blanket and I knew that someday this child would come to be in my care. And I knew I would wait as long as it took to find that child. I even knew the name of the child. I tried to send messages to those in the shadow realm so they would know that someday, help would come."

"Melora spoke of how you came to her in a dream …" I whispered. She was one of Merlin's former students who played a pivotal role in helping Sydney in the books. "She knew about the prophecy because of her dreams. She knew Sydney was coming …"

"When I read that first manuscript Fern had written, and she'd somehow captured so much of what I'd dreamt, it was staggering. So much in that book validated what I believed for hundreds of years. When she told me the story had come to her in a dream, I knew Arthur was trying to reach out from beyond the shadow realm."

Claire broke in. "But how have you been able to stay alive all these years?"

"One of my dreams showed me where to find Sangreal, The Holy Grail. It was hidden deep beneath the Abbey. Joseph of Arimathea had brought the Grail to England when he founded his church. That first Church of England eventually became the Abbey. It was this story of Joseph of Arimathea that had sparked the search for the Grail in the first place. For over 600 years the Abbey monks had guarded the holy relic.

"In my dream, I was given a password—something that would convince the Abbot that my need was genuine. I went to him and told him my story. He allowed me to drink from the Grail. And I received the gift of immortality."

"If the Grail was hidden in the Abbey when Morgan created the shadow realm," I asked, "wouldn't a shadow Grail also be in Dark Avalon? Didn't Morgan's curse create a shadow of everything and everyone in Camelot?"

Sydney nodded, clearly wondering the same thing.

"That is true," Merlin answered, "but the Grail's purity made it impervious to Morgan's dark magic."

"So that's why we had to come back here to the real world to get the Grail, because there's only one," Sydney said, putting it all together.

"Exactly, Sydney! For centuries, I helped one Abbot after another keep the Grail out of the wrong hands. During World War II, I created the chamber in Chalice Gardens, adding the extra piece of security— Excalibur as a key. Hitler was obsessed with finding the Grail, and I feared if England fell, the Abbey wouldn't offer enough protection. Luckily for England, the Nazis never made it this far."

He took a deep breath. "I'd spent years watching and waiting, then, seventeen years ago, the sign I'd been waiting for finally appeared." Merlin closed his eyes, remembering. "I was on the footpath, walking down the Tor after watching the sunrise. It was a beautiful spring morning. The air was crisp with a hint of sweetness. Daybreak mist was just beginning to burn off as I passed through the field of buttercups above Dodd Lane. That's when I heard the crying." He paused, dramatically. "A baby crying."

We all looked at Sydney and I saw she had tears shining in her eyes.

"It was you, Sydney," Merlin said, gently. "I heard you."

Chapter 18

The only sound was the crackle of the fire in the hearth. "What happened next?" I blurted, making Claire giggle. Sydney didn't move.

Merlin continued. "The cry came from a grove of trees at the other end of the orchard, a hundred yards or so away from the path. I found a tiny baby, just born, wrapped up in a scrap of tie-dyed cloth. That same cloth now holds the Grail. I knew at once that you were the child from my dream.

"But who had left you there? I didn't know then and I don't know now. Some poor Glasto pilgrim, perhaps. Or maybe an angel brought you down from Heaven." He smiled, but Sydney's face had gone stoic. I could feel her trembling next to me.

"I took you home. I cleaned you up. Went to the market to get the necessary supplies, formula and such. I created a story about my son and daughter-in-law passing away to explain why an old man like me would have an infant in his care. The fib stuck. I filled in the blanks as the years passed, as you grew older and began asking questions. I probably should have told you the truth from the beginning, but I convinced myself the lie would protect you. I knew you would do great things one day. And so you have. And so you will continue to do them!"

Merlin smiled warmly at Sydney who was now weeping openly. "A long, long time ago," he continued, "I helped raise a child destined for greatness. I didn't have Sir Ector to help me this time, but I believe in you, just as much as I did Arthur."

"You'll always be grandfather to me," Sydney burst out, launching herself into his arms. Claire wiped tears from under her eyes, sniffling. Suddenly Mom popped into my head. I pictured her tossing and turning in her fever bed back in London. Tears pricked behind my eyes. I imagined Mom waking up, looking for us, gripped by fear. I thought about how great she'd been to me the day Fern died. I felt terrible for leaving her home sick, for taking her car. Maybe we should have just told her the truth. She might have believed us.

Hmm, yeah, probably not.

Merlin kissed the top of Sydney's head. "It was the hardest thing in the world for me to allow you to find your way into Avalon." He looked up at Fern. "I almost told you who I was a million times, but something kept me from doing it."

Sydney released Merlin from her hug and stepped back to look at his face, keeping hold of his hands as he continued. "It was as you said, Fern. Things had to happen the way they were supposed to. I couldn't influence you or the story. The story had to go down on paper your way, and only your way."

Fern considered this, tugging on one ear thoughtfully. "I see your point."

Suddenly, I remembered something. "Hey, Fern, how many pages did you write of Into the Faraway?"

She thought a moment. "About a hundred or so, why?"

Sydney remembered too, and dropped Franklin's hands, whirling toward Fern. "We have a problem. At the Gardens, Henderson had to read from the manuscript so we could find the Grail. But he didn't read anything after page twenty-four. And everything after that is blank. In your pages, did Modred show up at the Gardens to stop us?"

Fern shook her head slowly. "No. No, I didn't write that."

Sydney sighed. "What does that mean?"

"Could it be a mistake?" Claire asked. "Like when Fern made the copy of the manuscript, the pages didn't actually copy ..." Claire trailed off as Fern shook her head.

"Hmmm," Merlin murmured.

"You know, it was strange that I even decided to make that copy in the first place," Fern said. "Doonesbury was right, I never made copies."

We all looked at Doonesbury who threw up his hands. "You see? I wasn't lying!"

Fern went on. "I always felt like there was something magical about those original pages, straight out of my old Royal typewriter. But the break-in made me nervous. I thought it might be a fan trying to find something to auction off on eBay or something. But I'm sure it was Modred."

"So, why are those pages now blank?" Merlin mused, standing to pace in front of the windows.

Sydney moved to the couch next to Bedivere. "I don't suppose you wrote Henderson into the story, did you, Fern?"

Fern shook her head.

"Modred was following Henderson and Claire," Merlin said, his voice bright, like maybe he was putting the pieces together. "He followed them to Glastonbury and then he followed us to the Gardens. And because he did, he found out about the Grail. When you appeared to Henderson, and asked him to help you, that changed the story."

"What if it's the Grail that's changed things?" Fern suggested. "Think about it. It's been since you had it in hand that Henderson no longer needed to read the manuscript. Could the Grail's magic allow Henderson to actually live the story? Eliminating the need to read it?"

We all fell silent. Fern turned to me, like she'd suddenly remembered something. "Henderson, before Bedivere took ill, you were going to tell me about that worry rock of yours. Where did you get that?"

I paused. "Worry rock?"

"You know," Fern said, frustrated. "Something small that you hold and 'worry.'"

I reached into my pocket, but I felt nothing solid. Panic scrambled up my throat. "No! No, no, no! What happened?"

My lucky rock had disintegrated. I dug into my pocket and pinched up as much of the rubble as possible, putting it into my palm.

"Lucky rock? What are you talking about?" Sydney asked.

"Henderson, answer me. Where did you get that rock?"

"I found it ..." The words struck home just before they made it to my lips. Why in the world hadn't I thought about that hidden compartment in my closet before now? All that stuff in there. I'd always wondered if it was Fern's? "There is this hidden compartment in the back of my closet. I discovered a box inside it, right after we moved in." Fern stared at me, her hand going to her necklace again. "Was it yours?" My voice cracked.

She smiled. "Honestly, I'd forgotten all about it. But yes, I hid my precious things in that secret cubbie." Her words crackled with excitement, like I'd just given her great news. "That's the connection! That silly little rock."

"What are you two talking about?" Sydney asked, looking back and forth between us.

"When I was a little girl," Fern said, floating closer to me, "I was obsessed with the Arthur legends. When I was thirteen, I begged my parents to take me to Glastonbury. We visited the Tor, of course, and that was the first time I saw the Living Rock. I didn't know the legend about it then, but I sensed there was something special about it. There were small pieces on the ground around it that had crumbled over the years, just sitting there. I took a couple home with me, as a keepsake. I wanted to have such a special part of that mystical place close to me all the time." She held up her necklace. "My mother had the smaller one made into a necklace for me. I never took it off."

My heart was pounding so hard I could barely breath. "It was a piece of the Living Rock?"

"Yes."

"You wore a piece of the Rock and I carried around the other piece."

"Yes!"

I looked down at my hand. "And now it's dust."

"Each of you kept a piece of the Living Rock on your bodies," Merlin said. "That gave you a physical connection along with a metaphysical one. Very interesting." He moved closer, examining the remnants in my hand.

"What happened to it?" I moaned.

Merlin put out his hand. "Here, let me try something." I transferred the dust into his palm and he took it to the kitchen. I exchanged a look with Claire and Sydney, then we followed him. Merlin sprinkled the dust into the dirt of a small potted plant that sat on a window sill over the sink, the dark window reflecting Merlin's craggy face. "I have a theory." He brushed the last of the dust from his palm. "Maybe you didn't need the Rock anymore, Henderson. Maybe it's the Grail, maybe it has to do with Modred, I don't know. But somehow, you've become part of this story now. Initially the Rock may have helped connect you with Fern's written story as you read it. And maybe her spirit was drawn to you because of it, in order to finish the story. But why else would the Rock just crumble like that? Maybe the story doesn't have to be written anymore to happen."

"But, how can the story be finished if we don't write it?" I asked.

"By living it," Fern said, nodding. "Yes, perhaps that is why those pages turned blank. You have all three elements to save Arthur: the Scabbard, the Grail, and Excalibur." She clasped her hands together and touched them to her mouth. "Oh, I so wish I could go with you tomorrow morning. To see Avalon, to actually be there—"

"Wait, what?" My heart skipped a beat. "Who's going where?"

"Fern is right," Sydney said. "We have to go back through the Doorway." She sounded so matter-of-fact, like traveling to another dimension was as normal as going to school.

"We who?" I asked, not wanting to hear the answer. A glance at Claire's terror-stricken face told me she suspected the answer.

"We us, of course!" Sydney sounded a bit put out.

"But I can't—"

"Henderson," Merlin said, gently, "You are a part of the story now. I'm not even sure they'd be able to get back through the Doorway without you."

"Well, they need to try?" I screeched, terrified. This wasn't part of the plan, not at all. I was just supposed to get the manuscript and the typewriter and go home. That was all I was supposed to do. It was getting close to midnight and my mom had no idea where we'd gone, and I was exhausted.

"Henderson. I understand this is scary," Fern said. "But Sydney needs you to save Arthur."

Sydney looked at me, expectantly. She probably thought I was a total crybaby. I blinked furiously. There was no way I was going to have Sydney Wakefield thinking about me like that. No way. I had to suck it up and be brave.

"All of us need to go?" I looked at Merlin for confirmation.

"You. Sydney. Bedivere. I cannot," Merlin said quietly, and Sydney whirled on him.

"But, you have to come! We need your power!"

"I'm sorry, my dear. Morgan made it impossible."

We all knew that was true. Then all eyes turned to me. "I'm sorry, too," I said, shaking my head. Claire moved close, slipping her hand into mine, her hands trembling. "But I can't go. I just can't."

Chapter 19

I lay on the floor of Merlin's flat, a pillow under my head and a soft grey blanket over my chest. I stared at the ceiling as rain pattered against the windows. I tapped my phone to check the time. 1:00. I didn't see how I was ever going to sleep. I was too busy beating myself up.

Why was I so scared all the time? Courage just wasn't something I had a lot of. I'd never been a big risk-taker; never wanted to ride skateboards or sneak out my bedroom window like I guess boys are supposed to do. Playing it safe just seemed so much more logical. Talking myself, and then Claire, into making this little trip out to Glastonbury was a big deal. I would never do something like this. And, honestly, I felt like I'd done enough. More than enough. Going into another realm, especially a shadow realm like Dark Avalon, was not part of the deal.

I could tell Sydney thought I was a loser; I saw it in her eyes. I even think Claire was disappointed, despite her obvious terror over the idea. She said she would go with if that's what I decided, which kind of blew me away. She and Bedivere had exchanged a long look when she said that. Too long a look if you ask me.

We'd agreed to stay until morning, since it was so late, and see off Sydney, Bedivere and a reluctant Doonesbury before making the drive back to London. Mom would be up and ready to ground us for the rest of our lives, probably, but it was better than Claire trying to drive home in the dark when we were both so exhausted.

Fern and Merlin hadn't pressured me on the matter, and for that I was grateful.

Now, I needed to sleep. I focused on the sound of the rain. It lulled me into a stupor and let my exhaustion win out. My eyes grew heavy, and finally, I couldn't keep them open anymore.

And then, I was dreaming.

Yep. One of those dreams.

I was standing on top of the Tor, looking down over Glastonbury. I wore only a short-sleeved shirt and the wind chilled my arms. I walked across the top of the grassy hill and went into the Tower to get out of the wind. I looked up at the two arched doorways on either side of the Tower. There was the one I'd walked through and the other was about nine or ten paces across the floor on the opposite side of the tower. The wind whistled across the hollow roof like a giant blowing across a Coke bottle. It made a deep moaning sound as swirling grey clouds sped by overhead.

I could sense the history of that Tower; the years that had passed through it. The ground tingled beneath my feet, as if an energy I couldn't begin to understand pulsed inside the hill itself.

I wasn't alone.

"You must be brave, young Henderson Green," a voice said, and I whirled to find myself standing next to a tall, bearded man wearing a deep purple cape that trailed on the ground behind him. He had a gold circlet crown on his head that wove an intricate pattern across his forehead.

Arthur. Who else could it be?

I couldn't speak, which seemed fine since he was doing all the talking anyway. "I know how difficult this is for you, but you must be strong. I need your help. Sydney and the others will not succeed without you by their side. While they have all the elements necessary to wake me, they cannot get to me if you do not accompany them."

I wanted to protest, to tell him I wasn't the hero in this story: Sydney was. But I couldn't make the words come.

"I know you worry for your mother, and you are of good heart to do so. But let me assure you, she is well. She will understand. Everything has happened as it should, and has been necessary to bring you to this point, Henderson. Leave fear behind. Feel the Knight within you. Stand firm against the evil created by Morgan and Modred. You are greater than it all!"

My mouth worked like a fish but still, no words. Arthur smiled down at me, putting a solid hand on my shoulder. "Wake now. It is time for you to come to Avalon. Be strong. Be brave."

And then my eyes opened. The fire in Merlin's hearth was nothing but smoldering embers. All was quiet. Fern hovered by the window, watching raindrops slide like tears down the windowpane. Ghosts didn't need to sleep.

I got up from the floor to stand next to her, and together we looked out over the dark, quiet street. "I think the rain is stopping," she whispered.

"Fern," I said quietly, my voice quavering as much as the rest of me. "I just had the most amazing dream."

She looked at me, a spark of hope in her eyes. "What kind of dream?"

"I think you know."

"Yes?"

"Arthur was there. We were in the Tower on top of the Tor. He told me I had to come to Avalon, that Sydney and Bedivere needed me." I closed my eyes and shook my head. "Oh man, I can't believe this is actually happening. I can't believe I'm actually agreeing to do this." My head spun and I sank into Franklin's easy chair.

"So, I guess I'm going then." My voice shook.

"Are you sure?" Fern asked, her smile hesitant.

"No. Not sure at all. Not one single little bit. But I'm going. I hope Claire will go, too."

"Somehow, I don't think you'll have trouble convincing her," Fern grinned, looking over at where Claire had snuggled up next to a sleeping Bedivere.

I paused. "Hey Fern? I know you're angry with Merlin and all, but he seems to understand how this is all supposed to play out, and he truly cares about you. He wouldn't have let something happen to you on purpose …"

"I know, Henderson. I'm not angry anymore. Truth is, I realized something last night. Something I suppose I've always known, but never allowed myself to believe. Not just about Franklin's identity. But about myself as well."

She turned from the window and looked at me, gently, like my mom sometimes did. "Even though the story has always felt very much a part of me, I've always believed I was just the storyteller. But I'm wondering if maybe there's more to it. And I just, well, forgot."

Before she could explain, Merlin appeared in the bedroom doorway, his expression tight. "It is 5 o'clock," he said, quietly.

It seemed like just seconds ago it was one in the morning and I was trying to go to sleep. I swallowed hard and took a deep breath.

It was time to go.

Avalon was waiting.

CHAPTER 20

The rain had stopped and the sky swirled with dark grey clouds. A faint glow in the eastern sky was the only indication morning was coming. We parked in the Chalice Gardens car park and walked down Chilkwell Street to Wellhouse Lane by flashlight. A quick left then a right and we were climbing a wide, steep sidewalk that stretched out before us beneath a canopy of dripping branches. Soggy brown leaves littered the walk with muddy blobs.

We reached a turnstile, where tourist information signs told us about the restoration of St. Michael's Tower and explained the significance of the Tor in Glastonbury history. Pushing through the swinging gate, we found ourselves on a narrow footpath.

It didn't take long for my heart to start hammering hard in my chest and the panting to begin. Excitement already had my pulse galloping, but the climb was a serious workout. We trudged up the first section until we came to a fence with another turnstile. After passing through it, we found the next section of hill was, unbelievably, even steeper. The sky had lightened during our hike, enough that we switched off the flashlights.

"There it is," Sydney wheezed, and I was glad I wasn't the only one having difficulty. "Right behind that bench."

The bench in question was occupied. Fern, waiting for us. "Hurry," she warned, "the sun is almost up!"

She was right. The sky smoldered with the promise of daybreak.

"We're coming already," Doonesbury gasped, and I wasn't surprised that the small, squat man was having trouble. I was a young kid in pretty good shape, but even for me it was a rough haul.

Merlin had come along to send us off. He and Fern looked at each other and I could tell he was hesitant. She smiled and nodded as if to say all was fine. Merlin's mouth turned up at the corners. I was relieved to see them back on good terms. "Ah, here we are!" he said, clapping his hands together and rubbing them like he was warming them over a fire.

"Yes, here we are," Claire said, sounding terrified. She was surprised to hear that I'd changed my mind about coming along on this insane adventure, but when she heard about my dream she wasn't about to be left behind. I grabbed her hand and squeezed. She squeezed back so hard she nearly broke my fingers.

"Jeez, sis," I grunted. "Ease up! I might actually need all ten fingers!"

Claire gave me a feeble, apologetic smile. She swallowed hard and whimpered. "Why, oh why, did I let you talk me into this?"

"Because you wanted to be the first girl in the 12th year to visit a shadow realm?" I raised an eyebrow.

"I just hope we live to tell about it," Claire gulped. "If we don't, I'm going to kill you!"

I snorted, laughter dowsing some of my fear, and squeezed her hand again. "It's going to be fine. After all, we're with one of the bravest knights of the Round Table," I nodded to Sir Bedivere who stood on Claire's other side, Excalibur strapped around his waist. He did look quite impressive, tall and gallant. His gaze fixed on Claire. I felt her hand relax in mine.

Oh brother. Do not tell me she's hot for a guy who lived 1500 years ago.

"Somehow, I think he's going to make a point of protecting you," I muttered.

"That I will, my lady," Bedivere said, touching the fingertips of his right hand to his forehead and bowing deeply. "It will be an honor to accompany you on this most momentous day. It is one I have long prayed for. Although I know not what will happen to me in the aftermath, I feel blessed to have known such brave young souls as Sydney and yourselves. You are all true sons and daughters of Camelot."

Claire practically swooned, gazing up into his eyes like a drooling idiot. I had to admit; his words were pretty inspiring. Part of Camelot. Me? I hoped to live up to that image.

Actually, I hoped just to live.

"Wait!" Sydney blurted. "Wait a minute! I almost forgot!" She ran off into the thicket of trees to our right.

"What is she doing?" Doonesbury whined. He was a big ball of panic just ready to pop like a hot dog in a microwave.

Sydney wasn't gone long, returning with a large white shield, its red dragon emblem peppered with arrow holes. "This might come in handy again," she said, giving it to Bedivere, who quickly strapped it on his back.

"Indeed. Good thinking."

"Why don't we join hands," Sydney suggested, keeping a close eye up the Tor, waiting for the sun to peak over the crest of the hill. "I've only done this at sunset, so I hope it works as well at sunrise."

I hadn't considered what would happen if the magic didn't work. What if we couldn't get through the doorway?

Claire quickly seized the opportunity to grab Bedivere's hand. I adjusted the pack on my back before holding out my left hand to Sydney, who stood next to the larger of the two broken pieces of stone. She laced her fingers through mine and a spark seemed to travel up my arm. She gave me a reassuring smile, then turned to Fern who floated up in front of her.

"Fern, you are the closest thing I ever had to a mother," she said. "I wish you could come with us. Do you think you could?"

"I don't know," Fern interrupted. "I will if I can. But even if I can't, part of me will always be with you. Right here." She reached out a ghostly finger and tapped Sydney's chest. "And you'll be in mine. Good luck, darling girl."

"Here comes the sun!" Merlin called, making me think of that Beatles song and I found myself giddy with nervous laughter. What was I doing?

Bedivere reached for Doonesbury's hand, but the little man backed away.

"Come, man, the time is nigh!" the Knight warned.

"I can't do it," Doonesbury trembled. "I just can't do it. I can't go with you."

"Sydney, now!" Merlin shouted, turning our attention away from Doonesbury. "Focus on the Doorway."

As soon as the words were out of his mouth, the sun crested and warm, orange sunlight spilled down over us. Sydney slapped her hand to the stone, and the rock began to glow red.

"It's working!" she cried, and I could feel the tingle of magic running from her other hand into mine, up my arm and down to Claire's fingers. The charge seemed to pass through her and then into Bedivere. His eyes lit up with determination.

I saw Bedivere reach out for Doonesbury again, who shrank back. I understood his fear. I was so terrified I could barely keep my knees from giving out. But I was a kid and Doonesbury was a grown up. For a fleeting moment, I wondered about Doonesbury's loyalty to Fern. I thought about the things Modred had said in the Garden the night before.

But before I could think too much about that, Bedivere threw back his head and hollered. "For Arthur!" His battle cry traveled up the hill toward the mist that hovered just beyond the Rock. There was a sudden roaring, like the sound of a huge waterfall. Then the mist rippled and a dark split appeared in it.

"Look at that," Claire marveled.

"Godspeed to you, my friends!" Merlin shouted over the roar. "I'll be waiting!"

Sydney ran for the Doorway, pulling all of us along. "We have to hurry," she cried. We ran, hand in hand, up the hill. We hadn't taken more than a few steps when I felt a pulling sensation in my gut and running was no longer necessary.

I felt dizzy, nauseous, and deliriously happy all at once.

Then we were through.

We tripped over each other, tumbling to the grass, landing in a heap.

As we untangled ourselves I glanced up and saw we were still on a hill. At the top, however, did not stand the ruins of St. Michael's Tower, but a castle unlike any I'd ever seen.

Camelot.

Chapter 21

"Well, it doesn't exactly look like the castle at Disney World," Claire muttered, brushing the dirt and grass from her clothes.

"Course not," I said. "That is a 6th century hill fort. The castles you're used to seeing are based on ones from medieval stories. Those kinds of castles were built hundreds of years later. King Arthur would have built one with wood and stone." I pointed up the hill. "Like that one."

"Thank you very much for the history lesson, Henderson, but we should really get out of sight," Sydney grinned, elbowing me in the ribs. "See those ramparts? The guards have a pretty clear view of this hillside. Come on! This way!"

I looked around for Fern, but there was no sign of her anywhere. My heart sunk. It would have been helpful to not only have her moral support but we sure could have used her ability to materialize whenever and wherever we needed her to. She would have made quite the lookout.

We'd left a beautiful morning back in our world for a grey wintery day in the shadow realm. The sky was cloudy and overcast, the sunrise devoid of the colorful glory we'd left behind on our side of the Doorway. Sydney grabbed hold of my hand again and pulled me toward a grove of trees further up the hill. I felt my face flush red, and not just because I was sweating my guts out. I'd go anywhere as long as Sydney had hold of my hand.

I knew from the Sydney Wakefield books that this hill was not the one the Tor stood on, but the hill in Cadbury, a few miles down the road from Glastonbury. In our time, the hill was empty, but some people believed it was once the location of Arthur's castle, Camelot. Maybe it was true, because it sure did in Morgan le Fay's Dark Avalon.

Claire and Bedivere followed close behind us. "Do you remember the way to Melora's hut without Gavin and Isabelle?" I asked Sydney.

"If I can find the tunnel entrance, then I think I can find the hut," Sydney answered. "That's the only way I've ever gone." We moved through the maze of trees as quietly as possible, pushing aside the heavy branches, holding them for the person behind. It was slow going. Beneath our feet, twigs and leaves crackled despite our caution. We had transferred the Grail and the plastic bottles of Chalice Well water to a leather pouch more befitting the time period than my school pack, and I felt the heaviness of the Grail in the pack—its weight a comfort. Surely we had Heavenly magic on our side with the Holy Grail in our possession, right? We couldn't lose.

Could we?

Sydney stopped and looked around, unsure. "I thought the tunnel would be right around here somewhere, but it all looks the same. Bedivere, does anything look familiar to you?"

He looked past her, through the trees. More than once, they'd escaped this castle through the tunnels running through the hill beneath it. Gavindale and Isabelle, Melora's kids and more of Merlin's pupils in the real world, worked in the castle and had shown Sydney the secret passages in Doorway to Avalon. It was under their escort that Bedivere and Sydney had made it through the forest before.

"Look, this tree," Bedivere said, putting out a hand to stop Sydney. "Do you recall this marking?" Someone had carved two intersecting circles into the trunk of a thick oak tree. It was the same shape of that pool in Chalice Gardens.

"Yes, that's right! Here is the path. Good thing you saw that, Bedivere. It's easy to miss."

Calling it a *path* was giving it a bit too much credit. It was more like a slight break in the trees. The ground did seem walked upon and some of the branches were cut back, allowing us to push through them more easily.

Still, we fought the underbrush for at least ten minutes before Claire asked, "Is it much farther?" She had scratches on her cheeks and forehead where loose brambles had scraped her. It felt like I had a few of those myself.

"We should be close, I think. Ouch," Sydney said as a branch snagged her hair. She quickly untangled it and we went on.

Minutes later, we emerged into a small open grove where a dilapidated hut stood near a circle of stones surrounding a smoldering pile of embers. It was amazing how well Fern described these places, none of which she had ever actually seen. But Melora's hut was just as I'd pictured it.

There was a scene in that first book where Melora told Sydney how she had apprenticed with Merlin in her real life. Here, in the shadow realm of Morgan's Dark Avalon, Merlin often came to her in dreams. In one of those dreams, he told her that someday a girl from the other world would come to save them. They called the real world The Faraway. Merlin had told her that this girl would save them all from Morgan's curse. Melora even knew the girl's name. This was known as Merlin's prophecy.

Sydney cautiously approached Melora's hut. It looked like it was made from groups of thin tree trunks laced side-by-side to form the base, then covered with grassy mud and topped by a thatched, cone-shaped roof.

A girl about Claire's age burst through the hut's doorway, tying a scarf around her head as she came. She froze, standing at the top of the two stone steps beneath the door. "Sydney! Praise the Heavens."

"Isabelle!" Sydney cried and the girl leapt down the steps to hug her. "It's good to see you!"

"You were successful then?" the girl asked, breathless. "You found Excalibur?"

Bedivere drew the Sword from the Scabbard in answer as a teenage boy who looked to be a bit older than me, but not as old as Claire, appeared at the entrance of the hut. "Mother!" the boy called, jubilant, "they're here! And they have the Sword!"

We all gazed at Excalibur for a moment, its brilliant blade shining despite the misty light barely seeping through the heavy ceiling of branches.

An older lady followed the boy out of the hut. "Sydney! Bedivere! You were successful?"

"It was with your wise guidance, Melora, that we were able to recover the Sword," Bedivere said, bowing his head in respect. "But it was with the help of your former teacher that we were able to obtain the third element."

Melora clapped her hands together. "Oh, Merlin! I knew he was watching over us."

Nobody seemed to have noticed Claire or me yet. It was kind of like I was watching a movie, only from the inside. Then Melora turned toward us.

"Now, who have we here?"

Sydney moved to my side and put an arm around my shoulder. "They are from The Faraway. They helped us find the Grail."

"The third element is the Holy Grail?" Gavindale blurted, as Isabelle collapsed to her knees. "The Chalice? But how?"

"We couldn't have done it without this one." Sydney gave my shoulders a squeeze and I felt my cheeks grow warm. "This is Henderson Green, and his sister, Claire. When I returned to The Faraway, I learned the reason the story was coming to life here. Henderson was making it happen as he read it. He has a connection with my friend Fern, the author." Sydney looked at me. "I still don't quite understand exactly how it works, but it does. If he hadn't read about me coming to Avalon, or returning to The Faraway for that matter, none of this would have happened."

Melora looked at me curiously, like I was an exhibit in a freak museum. "And now he is in the story?"

"Yes!" Sydney blurted. "Now the story doesn't have to be read anymore because Henderson is a part of it, we think so!"

We all took in that amazing idea. I still hadn't wrapped my mind fully around it, and every moment we'd spent here in Avalon felt surreal and strange. Like a super vivid dream that, somehow, was real.

"You must change what you wear." Melora flicked a hand in our direction. "But first, we eat. Then we plan, and then we wait. Once darkness falls tonight, we will return to the castle and finally do what we've dreamed of doing for so long. Finally, we will free the King!"

Chapter 22

I ended up wearing a pair of scratchy britches and a worn, yellow tunic. Both were too large for me, but luckily the baggy look was as much the style back then as it was at home. Claire fared a bit better in one of Isabelle's outfits—an ankle-length, dingy white dress with a dark brown, high-waisted pinafore. Isabelle wrapped Claire's hair into the same kind of a scarf she wore. We both looked very Arthurian, and I had to laugh. This was the ultimate in cosplay.

Even Bedivere approved, He held out a hand to Claire as she stepped out of the hut, gazing at her like she was a princess.

"Poor Ian," I murmured in Claire's ear. "Dumped for an older guy. Fifteen hundred years older."

"Cut it out! Bedivere is just being protective." Claire gave Bedivere a smile that made her seem regal, despite her shabby clothes. This time period suited her. Well, except for her shoes.

"Yeah, I don't think they wore those back in the sixth century," I said, pointing to her black boots.

Claire shrugged. "Isabelle's feet are too small." She dropped her voice to a whisper. "And I'm NOT wearing Gavin's boots. You should smell those things! Disgusting."

She was right. I knew because I currently wore a pair. They were a bit large, and floppy on my feet, but I'd have to deal since the alternative was going barefoot. Claire's boots barely showed beneath her skirt. Maybe no one would notice.

After a breakfast of cold broth and bread, which tasted amazing because we were so hungry, we sat in the hut to wait out the day. I could tell Sydney and Bedivere were anxious to be on their way to the castle, but it made sense to wait until dark. Melora explained that, during the daytime hours, the courtyard that held Arthur's glass coffin was filled with merchants and shoppers. Oh, and guards. We definitely wanted to avoid an encounter with them, and since Modred now knew we had the Grail, he would probably be watching and waiting for us to make a move.

The plan seemed good to me. I wasn't at all ready for a siege on the castle. I still couldn't believe I was actually in Avalon, hanging out with people I used to know only as fictional characters.

I also kept thinking about Mom. Time didn't pass the same here as back at home, in The Faraway, I knew that. But even so, by time we'd gone through the Doorway, it was morning. We'd been gone overnight. Mom had to be awake by now, and frantic. Out GPS tracking was off, although neither of us had received a text from her that morning. That made me wonder if she was okay. Was her fever worse? What if she was in the hospital or something?

I couldn't worry about that now. I had to focus on tonight's mission.

Isabelle was gathering wood and Gavin had left with his bow and arrow in search of a rabbit or two for supper, which kind of grossed me out but I wasn't feeling another meal of soup and bread either. Melora sat on a large stone near the hut sewing Gavin's shirt with something that looked like a piece of bone. Claire hung out with Bedivere as he stood guard by the entrance to the clearing. Sydney and I sat by the circle of stones, staring into the dead embers of last night's fire.

"I hate waiting," Sydney said, poking a skinny branch into the dusty ashes and giving them a stir. "I know why we need to, but it drives me crazy. We should have just waited until sunset at home before we crossed through The Doorway. At least then we wouldn't have to be so worried about getting caught out here in the woods."

I didn't like the thought of Morgan's guards combing the woods looking for us. "It's only a few more hours until sunset," I said, trying to reassure her. "Do you want to practice with the bow and arrow again?"

Before going off on his hunt, Gavin gave us a couple of wooden swords, and a bow and arrow to practice—just in case we ran into trouble that night. Sydney had given me some pointers with the sword that she had learned from Bedivere, which made me feel a little more confident in case I needed to defend myself. Then I tried to lift one of the real swords Gavin had lined up against the hut for me to take that night. They were crazy heavy. One of them was light enough for me to lift, but I couldn't imagine actually using it. I thought the bow and arrow would be better, but when I tried to shoot at the straw-stuffed target sack, I missed every time.

"You could definitely use a little more target practice," Sydney joked, poking me in the ribs with her elbow.

A flush crept up toward my ears. "I know, I'm going to be absolutely no help tonight." Why was I such a loser?

"Not true," Sydney said, her voice becoming more gentle. "You and I aren't here to fight our way to Arthur, anyway. It's my job to get Excalibur, the Scabbard, and The Grail across that magic circle barrier. It's your job to help me. Bedivere will take care of the rest."

The circle barrier. Its magic formed an invisible shield that no one except Sydney could cross. There were two of them we knew about— one was around Excalibur when it was hidden beneath the Tor, and another was around Arthur's glass coffin.

Now that Modred knew we had Excalibur, he and his mother would know we'd figure out how to cross her barrier. Which made me wonder if Morgan had rigged a different kind of trap in its place. I was about to say this to Sydney when Gavin burst through the underbrush in a panic. "Is Isabelle here?" he panted, desperate.

Melora stood, sewing tumbling to the ground. Her face had gone milky pale. "What happened?"

"Guards! On the north slope!"

"God in Heaven," Melora whispered, her hand trembling at her mouth. "Isabelle is there, collecting wood."

My heart hammered. If the guards caught her, would she lead them to us? I ran over to the hut and grabbed a small sword from the arsenal. This one was lighter than the other, but not by much. "We'd better get ready, just in case," I said, sounding braver than I felt.

Bedivere agreed. "Sydney, Henderson, take Claire into the hut and stay there. Melora, go about your business. Gavin and I will hide at the edge of the clearing. Gavin, be watchful!"

We quickly followed his orders. Sydney grabbed a sword for herself and we hauled the weapons inside the hut. It was dark and dusty inside, with a stone hearth against one wall. Near the opposite wall were two beds; just thickly stuffed pallets really, with no frame lifting them from the floor. The wooden floor echoed with every step we took. A rickety table was surrounded by three short stumps. Herbs hung upside-down in bunches around the edges of the cone-shaped roof. The top of the cone was open—to let out the smoke from the fireplace, I figured. There was one small window, a square cut into the branches that opened to the forest behind the hut.

I grabbed up the leather pack from the floor by the table, where I'd left it when we changed clothes. Slinging it on my back, I huddled next to Claire and Sydney behind the beds; the farthest point from the door. I imagined a hoard of guards bursting into the clearing, demanding Melora tell them where the Queen's traitors were hiding. I could picture them stomping into the hut, pulling us from our hiding places, Sydney screaming ...

I shook the images from my head. None of that was going to happen. Bedivere would protect us. And the Grail was in my pack. I could feel its heaviness against my back.

A calm settled over my heart. My breathing slowed. A confidence and bravery I'd never felt before enveloped my whole body. I don't know where it came from, but it felt good.

So what if the guards found us? We could take them. I had no doubt. I got up from my hiding place and walked to the door—basically just a rectangular hole curtained with a long piece of cloth.

"What are you doing?" Claire whispered, her voice harsh and biting. "Are you crazy? Get back here!"

"I'm just taking a look," I said, completely calm. "Chillax, okay?"

Sydney stared at me like I'd lost my mind. I fingered the hilt of the sword in my hand. Funny, it didn't feel as heavy as it had a few moments ago. I almost wished for the guards to show up. I'd show 'em a thing or two.

I peeked around the edge of the curtain and saw Melora sitting on her rock, sewing casually. The clearing was silent but for the sound of birds chirping in the woods. Then I heard a rustling as someone moved out of the brush and into the clearing. For a split second my mind showed me a guard, but then I realized it was only Isabelle, her arms overflowing with broken branches for the fire.

"Isabelle! Praise Heaven!" Melora burst, rushing to her daughter. "Are you all right? Did the guards see you?"

"What guards?" Isabelle asked, looking around. "Where is everyone?"

I jumped through the curtain, still holding out the sword. "Did they follow you?"

Isabelle glanced over her shoulder, her face worried. "Who?"

"The guards!" Melora and I said at the same time.

"What do you mean?" Isabelle protested, as Bedivere and Gavindale emerged from their hiding places. "I saw no guards."

Gavindale scowled. "Hopefully they didn't see you either. You must be more careful! Morgan's guards were on the hill near where you were gathering."

Isabelle turned a bit green. "You saw them?"

"You could have been captured!" Gavin warned.

His sister took a deep breath and seemed to gather her composure. "I'm sorry to have caused such worry. I assure you, everything is fine. Just fine." I looked at her. She seemed as nervous as a cat, not fine at all, actually.

Sydney and Claire poked their heads out of the hut. "Can we come out now?" Claire asked.

"The danger seems to have passed," Bedivere called, waving them out. "Apologies, Isabelle."

"All is forgiven," Isabelle murmured, her face still a bit pale. "One can never be too cautious."

Melora looked at her daughter, eyes narrowing. "Are you sure everything is all right?" she asked, reaching out and grabbing hold of her daughter's chin, turning her head for further inspection. "You look ill."

Isabelle yanked her face from Melora's grip with a scowl. "Mother, please. I am not a child. It is well, as I said. Do not worry."

Melora didn't look convinced to me, but she turned to Gavindale. "We still need meat for the meal. You sister is safe. Return to your duties."

Gavin nodded and slung his bow over his shoulder where it clanked against the quiver of arrows. "Yes, Mother." He raised one eyebrow at me and took off into the woods again. I wasn't sure what that look was supposed to mean. I went over to the hut where a ratty old sheath lay on the ground. I propped the sword against the wall, picked up the Scabbard and strapped it around my waist. Then I slid the sword into the sheath and felt the weight of it against my hip.

It was heavy, but I could handle it. It felt good.

Isabelle was safe. Just a false alarm. But the whole thing had changed something inside me. For the first time, I truly felt like maybe I was meant to be there. Like I really was part of the story.

I felt strong, brave, and ready for anything.

CHAPTER 23

"Getting into the castle will not be difficult," Melora said as we waited for darkness to fall completely. "Once we get past the courtyard guards. Knowing you now have the Grail, Morgan will no doubt have every guard on watch, day and night. We still have some advantage of surprise. They know we are coming but they do not know when."

Isabelle offered to refill our cups. She seemed nervous as she poured the water, but it was a rather nerve-wracking time. After a tasty dinner of roast rabbit, we were fed and ready to go, just waiting for Melora to give the word. She wanted to wait until the moon was high and the castle was asleep, which made sense when the element of the surprise was all you had going for you.

Melora went on prepping us. "Sydney, we know you can cross the magic circle Morgan conjured around Arthur's coffin. Let us hope Morgan remains confident in its power and has not altered it. Once we are in the courtyard, place Excalibur in its Scabbard on Arthur's chest. Then let him drink the water from the Grail. That should restore him completely."

Melora looked at me. "Once the curse is broken, Avalon will fall. Morgan was able to create Avalon only with the Sword and the Scabbard in her possession. She has lost them both, and keeping Arthur under her spell is all that now holds Avalon together. But once you awaken him ..." She trailed off, her eyes wet and shining. "You must get yourselves and Arthur back to the Doorway and out of Avalon before it is too late."

We all fell silent at that sobering thought. I hadn't put it all together, although I probably should have. Successfully rescuing Arthur would mean the end of Morgan's shadow realm. And that would mean that these people, who have known only this world, would cease to exist. The Melora, Gavindale, and Isabelle in the real world died hundreds of years ago. But these people, standing right in front of me, would be snuffed out along with Dark Avalon.

The night sounds of the forest enveloped us as the fire died down. I took a gulp of water and shivered. The thin tunic wasn't much against the cold night air, but that's not what made me shiver.

A few hours later, we followed Melora and her children back up the path, heading deeper into the woods, ducking under tree branches and brambles. It was slow going, especially for Gavindale, who carried a burning torch. I worried that someone in the castle could see the light, but Melora assured us the overgrowth was too thick. I couldn't see the castle above us, but I swore I could feel it lurking up there in the misty darkness.

The journey through the woods seemed to take forever, and all of us were weary and covered with scratches by the time we came to a mossy, vine-covered hill. "Here's the entrance to the tunnels," Sydney whispered. "There's an entire network of them beneath the hill fort. Isabelle has a map, but she and Gavin know these tunnels so well they don't even need it anymore."

"Don't Morgan and Modred know about these tunnels?" I asked.

"Oh, yeah, they know. These same tunnels were beneath the castle in the real world. Apparently Modred used them all the time to spy on Guinevere. That's how he found out about her and Lancelot."

"Ahhhhh." I remembered how in the second book, Sydney discovered Lancelot and Guinevere don't have shadows in Avalon because they were too far away from Camelot when the Arthur "died" and the spell was cast—Guinevere at the nunnery and Lancelot banished to France.

"So, if they know about the tunnels, won't they suspect we might use them to get into the castle?"

"There are hundreds of these passageways in and out of the castle. It would be impossible to guess which one we would use, or when," answered Gavin. He stepped forward, pulling aside a handful of long vines revealing a yawning hole in the side of the hill. "Ready?" he asked, holding his flaming torch high. Without a word, we followed him inside.

The ceiling of the tunnel wasn't very high and Bedivere had to hunch over to keep from banging his head. It was just right for the rest of us and we quickly moved through the musty, dank-smelling passageway. Before long the stench of torch smoke took over, filling my nose and burning my eyes.

We followed the twists and turns like a conga line of rats in a maze. In some spots patches of skinny tree roots reached out of the walls looking like dead snakes, in others water dripped in puddles and soaked into the muddy floor.

The incline of the tunnel wasn't steep, but the switchbacks and turns were exhausting. I was about to ask for a rest when we reached a fork; the right tunnel ending in a short set of stairs. The earthen steps led to the ceiling and a door made of thick planks of dark wood. Gavin doused the torch in a bucket of water placed at the foot of the steps, plunging us into darkness. The only light was a thin line that seeped through the space around the door. I heard Melora whisper. "Silence, now. Absolute silence."

I put my hand on the hilt of the sword strapped across my hip and it gave me a shot of bravery. But I did wish Bedivere and Excalibur weren't all the way in the back of the line.

At Melora's signal, Gavin lifted the door. There was a small creak and the weak line of light expanded. Gavin climbed out first, then turned and helped his sister and mother through. Sydney was next, then Claire and I, followed by Bedivere. We found ourselves in a small room lined with shelves and lit by a single torch in a wall holder. Dust our entrance had disturbed drifted in its golden light. Kegs of something stacked to the plank-lined roof where roots and herbs hung in dried bunches. Chaotic heaps of potatoes and carrots filled one corner. Gavin kicked a couple of potatoes out of the way and gently lowered the door back into the floor, hiding it from view with a tattered rug.

This was the kitchen pantry where Isabelle worked in Doorway, the place where Sydney hid during her first escape. So that meant we were right over the dungeons.

I swallowed hard, my throat tight.

Nearby, in the courtyard, sat Arthur's glass coffin. We were so close!

The castle remained quiet as we snuck out of the pantry and crept down the hallway, single file. Torches cast eerie, flickering shadows against the walls, looking like ghosts or demons ready to drag us off for trespassing. All the doors along the hallway were closed, and I prepared for discovery if any of them burst open. I could hear Claire's ragged breathing behind me and knew she was terrified too. I tried to push the fear away. This wasn't a time to be chicken. Then I remembered something Mom had always said, that bravery was doing what needed to be done even though you were scared. I guess I was being brave, then. This thought gave me a little boost of confidence.

Through an arched doorway at the end of the hallway was a large room with a high ceiling. Melora stopped at the doorway, peeked around the corner, and then nodded back at us. All was clear.

We followed her into the enormous dining hall. Dozens of wooden tables formed a great square. One section of the square was made up of two high-back thrones. Grand banners of black and gold hung from the walls. Above us loomed a huge wooden chandelier with about a million candles, none lit. We crept across the empty room toward another arched doorway. This one opened into a larger hallway than the one outside the pantry, with benches and tables lining the sides. This hill fort might not have looked like Cinderella's palace on the outside, but inside it held no shortage of wealth or treasure. Golden serving ware and glowing candlesticks covered every surface. Richly embroidered tapestries hung on the walls. The ornamental rug ran the length of the hallway, muffling our footsteps. We reached a large wooden door with a heavy metal bolt running across its middle. Melora slid the bolt and slowly swung the door open, and we all cringed at the creak of hinges.

We'd reached the courtyard. The soft sounds of the forest filled the air. Moonlight spilled its milky blue glow over everything. The courtyard looked like a town square closed for the night, with stables and shops for doing castle business during the day. I could imagine blacksmiths pounding anvils, men loading and unloading bales of wheat, and merchants hawking their wares from stands loaded with fruits and vegetables.

And at the other end of the courtyard, just beyond a set of stables, stood an enormous glass coffin.

Arthur.

We all saw it at the same moment, and the entire group ran toward it, racing across the moonlit space, eyes on our prize. Only Melora fell behind.

I slowed to a jog as I reached the coffin, stopping just outside the chalky white circle, staring at the coffin. It glowed with an ethereal light that had nothing to do with Morgan le Fay and everything to do with King Arthur, of that I was sure. He lay stretched out on a stone bench inside the glass case, cape flowing to the floor, the circlet crown still on his head. Other than the fact that he was lying down, and still as a statue, he looked exactly as he had in my dream.

There wasn't a single guard about. I felt grateful for this. I should have felt concerned.

"Uh, HG?" Claire squeaked from behind me. I looked over my shoulder and saw utter terror on her face. She pointed to a spot behind me.

Oh no.

The sight of the harsh silhouette in a darkened doorway across the yard made my blood run cold. He'd watched us run across the yard, let us revel in our success, just waiting for the best moment to snatch it away.

Nobody moved as he stepped into the moonlight.

Melora finally caught up to us.

"Oh, dear," she said, panting. "Modred."

Chapter 24

He swaggered across the courtyard with a confidence that sucked the wind right out of my brave sails. With a casual wave of his arm, hundreds of guards materialized from behind the stands, inside the stable, even appearing on the balcony above us. They held swords, pointy ends toward us.

Not good.

I heard the metallic sound of Bedivere drawing Excalibur and, taking his cue, drew my sword as well. Gavin and Sydney also had swords in hand as Modred continued his smug approach.

"Bedivere the Brave?" Modred sneered. "Perhaps Bedivere the Brainless would have been better."

"Poor Modred," Bedivere scoffed, unbolting the Scabbard with his left hand. He handed it to Sydney as he stepped in front of us. "Your days as ruler of this false Camelot are nearing their end."

Modred stepped closer and a full beam of moonlight showed his face had aged years since the night before. The man who'd looked not much older than Bedivere when he challenged him at Chalice Gardens now looked three decades older. His hair was streaked with grey, his face had lost its youth. "Surely you must realize this victory is mine. You have failed your King once again. I am, and will always be, the true ruler of Camelot."

"You're a fake!" I blurted before I even realized what I was saying. "And so is this entire kingdom!"

Modred turned his sneer my way and I could tell my words did no damage. "Yet who lies in his coffin and who stands before you now?" He pointed the tip of his sword at Arthur's still form, and then spun the weapon in his hand, making a dramatic challenge.

"Not for long!" Bedivere growled. With one swift move, he flipped his shield in front of him and charged toward Modred. Their swords clanged together and sparks flew. Melora pulled us back out of harm's way, but there was another group of guards hovering nearby, ready to cut us off if we tried to run. All we could do was huddle at the edge of the courtyard, out of reach of the guards yet a safe distance from the battle raging near Arthur's coffin.

Swinging Excalibur with one hand, Bedivere was able to block Modred's blows with his shield. Without a shield, Modred couldn't protect himself, but he could use both hands to swing his broadsword for a stronger blow.

"No magic to protect you this time, is there?" Modred taunted. Bedivere ignored him, handling Excalibur effortlessly, like it was an extension of his arm. It took everything in me not to rush in there and fight alongside him, but Sydney's hand on my arm restrained me.

"Don't forget," she murmured, tapping the Scabbard at her waist. "Without the Scabbard Modred can be killed."

Of course. Bedivere had left it with Sydney, not wanting it to fall into Modred's hands. But even if Bedivere was successful in this fight, would that be the end of all this? Doubtful. We were surrounded by guards, after all. We needed to get Sydney inside the circle with the three elements. None of the guards would be able to touch her, then. Unfortunately, one of the elements was a little busy at the moment.

Bedivere tossed the shield aside, gripping Excalibur with both hands and draining Modred of any advantage. Excalibur clanged against Modred's sword again and again as Bedivere drove the fake ruler to his knees.

Some of the guards tried to move in for an assist, but Modred wouldn't have it. "Fall back! The swine is mine! I will bring this traitor down, Excalibur or no."

"Traitor?" Bedivere roared, a collision of steel sending sparks skittering across the ground. "The only traitor in this castle is you, ungrateful welp! I warned you this day would come. Soon you will feel the wrath of Arthur's anger. I look forward to seeing you beg for his mercy."

This comment seemed to really make Modred mad and he came back with three forceful swings. Bedivere dodged and parried. Then, swung Excalibur upwards, knocking Modred's sword from his hands. It clattered to the ground, sliding across the chalk line of the magic circle. Bedivere dipped down and spun, swiping a leg at Modred's ankles, knocking him off his feet. Before Bedivere could move toward him, the point of a sword was at his throat. He froze, cutting his eyes at the castle guard. "Go on, give me reason to drive you through," the guard growled.

Modred pushed himself up to sitting. "I win, and you lose. Now, hand over Excalibur, if you please."

"Sydney!" Bedivere dropped Excalibur to the ground and kicked it. It slid back to us and Sydney snatched it up. She ran for the circle, but skidded to a halt when a thin, older woman wearing an elegant dark green dress materialized directly in front of her.

Before any of us knew what was happening, the white-haired woman grabbed Sydney, spun her around and clasped one arm across Sydney's chest. My heart convulsed as she placed the point of a jeweled dagger to Sydney's throat. Excalibur dangled helplessly in Sydney's hand.

The woman moved like someone younger, but her face looked ancient, all wrinkled and shriveled.

It had to be Morgan le Fay.

"I see you brought your own army this time, pixie," Morgan cackled. "Too bad your coup will be a miserable failure." She pushed the point of the dagger against Sydney's neck, making her cry out.

"Sydney!" I yelled, lunging for her, but Claire pulled me back.

Morgan leered. "You took something that belongs to me, girl, and now you will return it!"

I had to help her, but what could I do? Then the weight of the pack on my back gave me an idea, remembering the intense feeling that had come over me when I'd first laid eyes on the Grail—I was awe-struck over its breathtaking light. Its otherworldly presence.

Slowly, I moved the leather pack off my shoulder and slipped my hand inside, my fingers wrapping around the cloth that held the Grail. I pulled it out, keeping the cloth wrapped tightly around it. Timing was everything here.

Morgan reached for the Scabbard, but it was slung too low on Sydney's hips. She couldn't get it without letting go of her grip on Sydney. "Drop the blade. Take off the Scabbard!" Morgan demanded, as a line of blood ran down Sydney's neck from the tip of the dagger.

It was now or never.

"Hey!" I yelled at the top of my lungs, ripping the cloth from the Grail and holding the Cup above my head like a trophy.

The miraculous light poured out over the courtyard like a Holy fountain. "Behold!" I yelled. "Arthur commands the power of the Holy Grail. All hail Arthur!"

I don't know where the words came from, but they sounded important and intimidating, so that was cool. A gasp rippled through the crowd. Some guards instantly dropped to their knees, but just as many fled or stood frozen and confused.

Claire elbowed me. "What are you doing?" she hissed. I ignored her, hoisting the Grail higher.

The initial reaction definitely made everyone pause, but then Morgan shouted. "The Grail! The boy has the Grail! Modred, the Grail will save us!"

I tried to run, but guards were on me immediately, one of them snatching the Grail from my hands. My plan had backfired. I'd hoped for a distraction, something that would allow Sydney to get away, but all I'd done was reveal the Grail's location. We were completely stuffed, as Colin would say.

Excalibur slid out of Sydney's hands and the mighty blade clanked in defeat against the cold stones. Bedivere looked at Arthur in his glass coffin, the King's eyes staring at the stars above, and bowed his head in shame. We had failed him. I had failed him.

Morgan re-sheathed her dagger and pushed Sydney back toward us. "You lead your army well, my dear. Right into a trap. And you!" She pointed at Isabelle. "You have earned your reward."

What?

We all turned toward Isabelle. Sydney's expression shifted from disbelief to fury. "You betrayed us! How could you?"

Isabelle dropped her eyes, then ran to a young guard, who pulled her into his arms around her.

"You traitorous, deceiving wench!" Gavin bellowed, and two guards grabbed him before he could attack his sister.

Isabelle burst into tears, her expression tortured. "You cannot understand! The Queen said she would kill Michael if I did not help her. I had no choice." Then she buried her head against the chest of the guard, Michael, I assumed.

Gavin wailed, his voice filled with as much pain as anger.

"We must not let this betrayal defeat us," Melora said, putting a hand on her son's shoulder. "She allowed fear to win out over truth, but it will not keep us from saving Arthur." Melora stood tall and firm. She faced Morgan, head high and proclaimed: "Surrender now, Morgan, and perhaps God will forgive you."

Morgan cackled and strode over to Melora. "I have the power here. Not God. Not Merlin. Not … Arthur," she spat his name. "Me!"

Then Morgan turned her sights on me. Her deep purple eyes sparked with crazy and her long white hair flowed like a river from her head. You could just feel the evil like a cloud around her. She took the Grail from the guard and smiled. "The magic of the Scabbard is nothing compared to the power this Cup contains. Once we drink from this, nothing can touch us. We will live forever! Where is the well water?" She nodded at the guard who grabbed my pack and pulled out the plastic bottles we'd filled at Chalice Well. Morgan snatched a bottle from him but, after a moment of struggling with it, she growled and thrust the bottle towards me. "Uncork this, boy!"

What choice did I have? I unscrewed the cap slowly, trying to come up with a plan. One that might work, this time. I had to prevent Morgan from drinking from the Grail, and there was only one way I could think of to do that. I'd already screwed up our chance to save Arthur, I sure wasn't going to be the one to help this old witch gain immortality.

I was about to dump out the water when I heard Merlin's voice in my head; something he'd said in the car on the way to Chalice Well.

"The Grail is a holy relic, and could only be found when it was to be used for good."

I knew exactly what to do.

I poured the water into the Grail, just as Morgan asked. "Henderson, no!" Sydney begged.

"It's okay, Sydney," I promised, hoping I was right about this.

I handed the Grail to Morgan. At the first sip, light seemed to flow through Morgan's body as the water flowed down her throat. I hoped I hadn't been wrong to trust that Merlin-voice in my head. But then, Morgan began to choke and cough green curls of smoke. She clawed at her neck, her face turned red, then black, swelling and bubbling with big bulbous boils.

"Mother!" Modred screeched in horror. I backed further away. Everyone watched, shocked, as Morgan le Fay melted away before our eyes.

"What's happening?" Claire screamed, unable to rip her gaze away from the scene.

"Morgan is evil. But the Grail … is good," I explained. "The two don't mix."

The queen's anguished scream echoed through the courtyard. The whole scene reminded me Dorothy throwing a bucket of water on the Wicked Witch of the West. Morgan melted like sugar although, clearly, she was made of something far less sweet and much more poisonous. Green tendrils of smoke filled the air as she disintegrated. The Grail tumbled onto the empty emerald dress.

"Nooooo!!" Modred screamed. He snatched a sword from a nearby guard and headed my direction. "You killed her!" He roared, a vengeful dragon.

This was not good. Not at all.

Bedivere wrenched himself away from the guard, grabbed his sword and stepped between me and Modred. They circled each other, eyes ablaze, and then the real battle began.

Swords whooshed so fast I could barely see them, sending sparks flying. Modred ducked, then lunged. Bedivere rolled out of the way. It went on like this for a while, but then I could tell that having drank from the Grail gave Bedivere an edge. Modred weakened, putting up a hand. Bedivere paused, sword still at the ready. "Do you surrender?" he asked.

Modred glared at him, but he didn't have the energy to protest. His face grew older, his skin sinking fast now. He dropped his sword, collapsed to the ground, and turned to dust.

Claire gasped. "He's gone!"

A gust of wind whipped through the courtyard, turning what was left of Modred into a dust devil that swirled away into the night sky.

Claire threw herself into Bedivere's arms, covering his face with kisses. "I'm so glad you're okay!" I was embarrassed for her.

I retrieved the Grail, thankful it hadn't broken. Guess it was made of tougher stuff than that.

"Sydney!" I yelled. "Go!" I didn't have to ask her twice. She slipped Excalibur into the Scabbard as we approached the chalk circle, where Arthur waited.

Then Sydney took a deep breath, and stepped across the line.

CHAPTER 25

Sydney stood before the glass coffin, looking down at Arthur. His purple cape pooled out across the floor. His eyes stared blankly upwards. I wondered if he was aware of what was happening, or if he was unconscious. I guessed we would soon find out.

Placing Excalibur on the ground, Sydney used both hands to lift the glass lid of the coffin. She grunted and groaned, raising it only a few inches before it slammed back into place.

"Don't break it!" I cringed, and without thinking, rushed to help her. "Are you okay?"

"How did you—" Sydney began, but Claire interrupted.

"HG, you crossed the circle!"

I looked back at the chalk line I'd stepped over without a problem. Bedivere moved forward and tried to join us by Arthur's coffin, but it was like he'd hit an invisible wall.

"Why can you both cross the circle?" he asked, frustrated.

I thought for a moment. "Fern wrote that Sydney can cross the circle because she's not of Avalon. Well, neither am I."

"And neither am I!" Claire echoed, stepping across to join us.

"Oh, thank goodness," Sydney breathed. "Here, help me with this!"

I crossed back over the circle to give the Grail to Bedivere, then helped Claire and Sydney slide the lid off the coffin. When it hit the stone floor, it cracked in a dozen giant pieces. Sydney unbuckled the Scabbard and lifted it with Excalibur inside over the wall of the coffin. She had to go up on her tiptoes to place it on Arthur's chest.

We all held our breath.

At first, nothing happened. Then Arthur blinked.

"Yes!" Sydney cried joyfully. I grabbed Claire in a mad bear hug and twirled her around. Then I did the same with Sydney. When I put her down she put a hand on either side of my face and gave me a big smack, right on the mouth. "Oh, thank you, thank you, Henderson Green! I couldn't have done any of this without you."

Kill me now, I thought, it doesn't get better than this.

Arthur didn't sit up or even move. His hands just clutched the Scabbard. "We need the Grail!" Sydney said.

I ran back to where Bedivere waited, holding the Cup. Retrieving it and the second plastic bottle from my pack, I ran back to the coffin. "Here, hold this," I said, handing the Grail to Sydney. I poured in the water, careful to not to spill a drop. "How are we going to get him to drink?"

"I dunno," Sydney admitted. "I'm making this up as we go along." Neither of us could reach his mouth with him lying down, so Sydney just grabbed the Grail and poured the water over Arthur's mouth. It spilled over his chin at first, but then Arthur opened his mouth and Sydney poured it in. Just like Bedivere, he gulped the water down. Sydney stopped pouring, but Arthur sat up. The Scabbard slid off his lap as he grabbed the Cup from Sydney, draining it.

A low rumbling sounded somewhere off in the distance. Something about it made the hair on the back of my neck stand up.

Arthur climbed to his feet, standing on the stone bench where for so long he lay—not dead but not alive, either. "Praise the Lord from whom this miracle has come!" he proclaimed, holding the Grail above his head. The Grail lit up, shining over the courtyard. The crowd erupted into an uproar of cheers. "Hail King Arthur!" I heard someone cry. "Praise be to God!" someone else shouted.

The low rumbling grew louder, drowning out all other sounds.

Melora waved her arms, shouting for attention. "Children, quickly! You must leave!" The ground beneath us vibrated and I remembered the warning Melora gave us earlier.

Once the curse is broken, Avalon will fall apart. It will be your challenge then, to get yourselves and Arthur back to the Doorway before Avalon succeeds in destroying itself forever.

"Sydney, we've got to get to the Doorway! Now!" I yelled. "Arthur! We have to get you out of that coffin!"

"Stand back!" Arthur replied. He handed me the Grail, which I quickly re-wrapped in Sydney's swaddling cloth, and returned to the pouch. We backed away as the rumbling grew more intense.

"Hurry, your Majesty!" Melora begged.

Arthur buckled the Scabbard around his waist then pulled out Excalibur, an expression of loving familiarity on his face. The Sword glimmered as if it was pleased to be back in the hand of the man for whom it was forged.

The huge blade swung down and shattered the glass coffin.

"Yes. That felt good." Arthur grinned, then strode over to Bedivere and embraced him strongly, oblivious to the shaking ground beneath his feet.

"You saved me, all of you. You have my undying thanks."

"We appreciate that, my liege, but Melora is right. Morgan's curse is broken and Avalon is coming apart. We must get you out of this realm or all will be for naught."

Melora grabbed Arthur's arm, gazing up into his face with such admiration and respect, it raised a lump in my throat. "You are the once and future King, my lord. The future we have prayed for has finally arrived." She looked at us, her eyes shining. "Thank you. Now run!" She shoved us toward the front entrance of the courtyard. "Run for your lives!"

I looked over my shoulder as we raced for the gate. Gavin and his mother wrapped their arms around each other, watching us go. "How can we just leave them?" I said, a huge lump in my throat making it hard to talk. Sections of the castle had fallen, huts had toppled over. The ground shook like crazy, splitting here and there, the cracks racing across the ground.

Isabelle rushed past us in the other direction. I turned and saw Melora throw her arms around her daughter.

"Henderson, come on!" Sydney yelled, pulling me through the chaos. They always knew it would come to this, I thought. They even seemed to wish for it. So, I shouldn't feel bad.

But I did. Terribly bad.

Arthur, Bedivere, and Claire lead the way through the front gate and onto the dirt road that wound its way down the hillside. The air had a peculiar sheen that made everything look plastic and false.

"How are we going to get down the hill?" Sydney asked, as we held onto each other, trying to stay on our feet. "It's so steep!"

"If we had a sled," Claire said, "we could just slide down."

It was a fantastic idea, but where were we going to get a sled?

"What about that?" Sydney yelled, pointing to a wooden boat. It looked more like a long canoe that seemed to be a work-in-progress, a thick log held up by two sections of stump. One end had been shaved smoothed like the prow of a boat but the back was still a raw tree trunk.

Arthur and Bedivere hauled the half-completed boat to the edge of the hill. The center had been carved out, and we climbed in. Claire sat behind me and Sydney in front.

"Get in, Bedivere," Arthur commanded.

"There is only room enough for you, my liege," Bedivere yelled.

"No!" Claire screeched, whipping around in the boat. "Bedivere, you have to come back with us! You drank from the Grail, you'll be fine now! Please!"

Bedivere took Claire's hand and smiled down at her. "As much as I wish it was not so, my life was over long ago."

"Claire, Bedivere is right," I yelled to be heard over the rumbling, hating every word.

Sobbing in protest, Claire buried her head in my back. Bedivere and I looked at each other. "Thank you, for everything," I said, reaching for his hand. We shook, then he touched Sydney's cheek tenderly. The ground heaved, nearly knocking us out of the boat.

"You have to go!" Bedivere gave Claire's shoulder a squeeze, then turned to Arthur. He dropped to one knee. "For my part in this, I am truly sorry."

"No, Bedivere, do not apologize. You are a true friend."

The ground bucked so hard it nearly knocked Bedivere off his feet. "Go!" he yelled.

The next thing I knew, we were careening down the hill.

CHAPTER 26

No amusement park ride was ever this wild.

We zipped down that grass at a mind-blowing speed, bumping over hillocks and rabbit burrows. Sydney and Claire screamed the entire way, but not me. If it weren't for the whole world-collapsing-around-us thing, it might have even been fun.

We reached the bottom in one piece, only yards from the Rock, the gaping Doorway open and waiting for us. Suddenly, the roaring sound morphed into a high-pitched shriek. The castle was caving in on itself. Avalon was imploding.

Leaping from the boat, Sydney grabbed King Arthur's hand, Claire grabbed mine, and we ran full out toward the Doorway. Behind us, an enormous sucking sound mixed with the high-pitched shriek and I knew without even looking over my shoulder that the entire realm was being erased.

We dove through the rip and tumbled across the grass of the Tor. I tried to get to my feet, but the ground shook so badly I couldn't. Thunder, or something that sounded like it, rolled across the stormy sky.

Sydney and Claire had just as much difficulty trying to stand. Sydney's gaze swept the hillside, eyes wide. "Where is Arthur?" she screamed.

I finally got to my feet, searching for any sign of the King. Up the Tor, St. Michael's Tower was crumbling, just like the castle in Dark Avalon.

Tourists ran, screaming, in all directions as chunks of stone fell like bombs. A mass of rabbits raced past us, hopping for their furry, cotton-tailed lives. People on the footpath, who hadn't yet reached the summit, slid down the grassy sides of the Tor, unable to keep on their feet but desperate to put as much distance between them and the Tower as they could.

Panic gripped me. "Where is Arthur?" Sydney screamed again.

"I don't know!"

Her eyes grew wide and frightened as she searched the hillside. "There!" She pointed at a spot near the top where Arthur's purple cape billowed in the wind as he climbed. He was halfway to the summit already. Speedy dude.

A mixture of rumbling and screaming filled the air. It felt like the world was trying to turn itself upside down and inside out all at the same time. People ran, people screamed, and one guy near the bottom of the Tor held up his phone like he was recording. If he survives, I thought, that video will be worth something.

Squinting in disbelief, I gasped. Was that … *Doonesbury*?

I swayed as another tremor shook the ground.

"Look!" Claire shouted. "Merlin is up there, too!"

I forgot all about the man who might be Doonesbury and searched the hilltop. There he was, standing at the edge of the summit, arms outstretched as if inviting God to strike him down.

"What is he doing?" I yelled. And then I realized that Sydney was on her way up the hillside, too. What was wrong with these people? "Sydney, no! It's too dangerous!"

"He's my grandfather!" she screamed over her shoulder without slowing.

"Then I'm going with you!" I yelled back, hoping this wasn't the stupidest thing I'd ever done in my life. My legs ached from the effort of moving up the steep hill while the earth tried its hardest to toss us back to the bottom.

Sydney had almost reached the summit. I looked back and saw Claire right behind me. I reached the top of the Tor and found Arthur and Merlin standing side by side, near the far edge. They were holding Excalibur horizontally between them, Merlin's hands on top of Arthur's, like he was blessing the sword or something.

They stood on the opposite side of the summit, fifty or so yards away from the tower. I prayed we wouldn't get beaned by falling pieces of tower as we raced by the trembling structure. A flat, circular stone, some sort of marker, was on the ground between them. Merlin encouraged Arthur to do something, but the rumbling was too loud for me to hear what he said. The ground heaved, sending me sprawling and knocking Sydney and Claire down in the process.

I looked up in time to see Arthur plant his feet and raise Excalibur high above his head. The Blade shimmered as he swiveled it, pointy end down, and then thrust it deep into the center of the stone marker.

The sparks that flew during Bedivere's battle with Modred didn't even compare to the fireworks as Excalibur seared a violent path through the rock marker, only stopping when the hilt hit the top. Instantly, the ground stopped shaking. The rumbling ceased. I held my breath, waiting to see if it was over for real. After a few moments passed, the crowd must have believed it because a cheer went up in celebration of their survival. Of course, they all thought it was some random earthquake. They had no idea.

Arthur stood next to the stone and Excalibur, an expression of pure relief on his face. Then, something off to our side caught his attention and he looked amazed, like he was glimpsing a bit of Heaven. Sydney and Claire noticed too. We all turned, following his gaze. And there, standing next to St. Michael's Tower, was Fern.

She was dressed differently than her normal jeans and blouse. Now she wore a long, flowing white gown with a crown of small, white flowers in her hair. But what made my heart stop wasn't what she wore. It was that she looked so … real. Like she was alive again.

Sydney gasped. Arthur moved toward Fern, his hands reaching out as if he feared she would dissolve before he could touch her. Sydney, Claire, and I crept closer too, desperate to hear their words.

"Arthur." Fern smiled and even her voice sounded different.

"It can't be …" Arthur said, visibly trembling. "Is it really you?"

"Yes, my darling, yes! Oh, Arthur, I remember. I remember everything!"

"All this time," said Arthur, almost to her now, "I hoped and prayed that one day I would see your face again. Although I slept not a wink in Morgan's realm, I did dream. Every day and every night. And all my dreams were of you."

"And you were in my dreams, too. I just didn't realize what they meant. But now I do."

Arthur paused, dropping his hand. "But, I thought you loved Lancelot."

"I did," Fern closed her eyes, like she hated saying those words. Then she looked at Arthur tenderly and walked toward him, hesitant. "At least, I thought I did. But I was wrong. I convinced myself you cared more for the quest than for me."

Arthur swallowed hard. "I was not the King you deserved."

"Oh, but my darling, no, it's not your fault. I was wrong. My love for you was the real love. Morgan's evil magic had infected everything. How could you ever forgive me, forgive Lancelot, forgive the betrayal? I couldn't bear it. And I prayed each day, until the day I died, that I would be given a chance to prove my love for you." Her eyes shined brightly, and there was a warm glow all around her now. "Through so many lifetimes, I've searched for a way, and I didn't even know it was happening. This time was different." She put out her hand and Arthur reached out to her again.

Sydney and I exchanged confused looks. "Are you understanding any of this?" Sydney asked, and I shook my head, completely lost.

"I think I do," murmured Claire. "Fern is Guinevere."

"That can't b—" I started to protest, then hesitated. "Guinevere? You think?"

"The one true love of Arthur's life," Sydney breathed.

"But how?"

Before we could debate it further, Fern's and Arthur's fingers finally met, and as their hands touched Fern's bright glow swirled around Arthur, enveloping him as well. He pulled Fern into his arms and she looked up into his face.

I held my breath.

"My dearest," Arthur whispered.

Fern looked so happy. "Finally," she breathed. "Finally."

The glow became solid and gossamer waves of brilliant red and gold swirled around them, binding them together, lifting them from the ground. A shaft of pure white light broke through the clouds, connecting the heavens to the earth. Arthur and Fern—no, Arthur and Guinevere—floated upward in that shaft of light, staring into each other's eyes, rising until we couldn't see them anymore.

The light faded away.

I felt hot tears prick my eyes.

"What. Just. Happened?" I choked out.

"They are together at last," Sydney whispered. "That's what this was all about, Henderson. Guinevere finding a way to make things right."

"That was intense," Claire said, staring up at the sky.

"Fern was Guinevere," I breathed, amazed. "All this time. We never knew."

"I don't think she knew," Sydney said. "It explains so much."

"Right?" Claire said. "It's why she was so obsessed about saving Arthur. Why she was so into the Arthur legends, even as a little girl."

I remembered the expression on Fern's face when I walked into my room and found her looking at the drawing of Arthur on the cover of Doorway to Avalon. Her expression was so sad, so full of regret.

Suddenly, Claire was hugging me. "I am so glad you talked me into coming to Glastonbury," she cried.

I laughed, wiped my eyes with the back of my sleeve. As sad as I was to know I would never see Fern again, it was awesome to think that her soul was finally at peace. And that King Arthur finally had his queen back.

Merlin came up behind us and clapped a hand on my shoulder. "Now that is what I call a successful quest," he said.

"Did you know, Grandfather?" Sydney asked, grabbing his arm. "Did you know she was Guinevere?"

Merlin's eyes shone, and he smiled. "Let's just say this is a miracle I've hoped would happen for many, many years."

"Hullo! Merlin!"

Doonesbury ran across the Tor's summit, waving his phone. "I got it all, every earth-shaking moment!"

"You recorded everything?" Merlin asked, raising an eyebrow.

"I even got them coming back through the Doorway! Do you know how much this will be worth?" Doonesbury gushed, waving the phone in front of Merlin's nose. "Millions! Millions, I tell you!"

"I don't think so, mate." Merlin shook his head in mock sadness.

Doonesbury hesitated, his enthusiasm dropping for a moment.

"Wha— why not?"

"Well, I think you might have accidentally erased the file," Merlin answered and Doonesbury's face fell even further.

"What are you talking about? I just told you—"

Merlin waved his hand over Doonesbury's phone.

"What did you do?" Doonesbury squeaked, frantically tapping his phone. "It's gone! How did you do that? Why?"

"You can't sell that video, Stanley."

"Why not? It's a gold mine!"

"It would spoil the ending, don't you see?"

"The ending?"

Claire and I exchanged a look and Sydney grinned, catching on.

"Of course!" Merlin said with a smile. "The ending of a very wonderful book."

CHAPTER 27

Sirens wailed in the distance as we made our way down the Tor. By time we got to the street, a mass of emergency vehicles had arrived. As disheveled and strangely dressed as we were, we didn't really stand out in the adrenalin-pumped crowd of people and onlookers.

"Henderson! Claire!"

Mom burst through the crowd, shoving her way past people to get to us.

"Mom!" Claire yelled, sounding like a kindergartner after the first day of school. Mom's expression was a strange mixture of rage and relief. I figured Claire and I would both be grounded until next summer, but I could try to smooth things over.

"Mom! You look like you're feeling a lot, um, better ..." Admittedly, it was a feeble attempt, one that was met with a look that told me her recovery just might be my downfall. Then the moment passed and she swept us both into a hug, tears flowing. I hated it when she cried. I'd rather have her yell.

"Don't you ever, ever, do that to me again!" she scolded through her sobs.

We promised we wouldn't ever, ever do it again, exchanging a glance over her shoulder. It would be an easy promise to keep.

"How did you know where we were?" Claire just had to ask.

"You didn't make it easy. Your tracking was off and you weren't responding to calls or texts. I thought you were dead in a ditch somewhere!"

I shot Claire a look and she narrowed her eyes at me. Mom went on. "I was about to call the police when Colin showed up at the door. Turns out he was pretty worried about you. He told me everything."

"Everything?" I asked, too quickly.

"I knew you were upset about Fern Caldwell's death, Henderson, but convincing your sister to drive you all the way out here so you could pay your last respects ... that was just dangerous. I would have driven you here, if you'd asked."

Such a clever one, that Colin. Told her just enough, without revealing everything.

"I'd been thinking about coming out here anyway. All the news reports about Glastonbury, got me thinking—" Mom froze, gaze directed over my shoulder. Claire and I both turned to follow her gaze to a woman about Mom's age, wearing an expression of total disbelief. A woman I'd seen the night before at Chalice Gardens, when she'd let us in to retrieve the Grail.

"Maggie?" said Mom, her eyes filling with tears again. "*Maggie!*"

We showed up at Chalice Gardens at dawn the next morning. We needed to be there before the Gardens opened to the public for the day because we had something very important to do. Something very secret.

Margaret—who also happened to be our long, lost Aunt Maggie— met us again at the front gate. She gave us a gigantic smile and hugged us like we hadn't just spent the entire last evening together as she and Mom cried and apologized and made up for lost time.

Over dinner, we'd found out it was Mom who had printed out the directions to Glastonbury, because she was thinking about driving out to look for Maggie. How they ended up in tucked in Claire's book, nobody knows. Maybe just coincidence.

We also heard the full story behind how Maggie ended up in Glastonbury.

We already knew Maggie came to Glastonbury on a post-college graduation trip. Obsessed with everything that had to do with Avalon, she felt she was destined to make contact with "The Goddess." Once she'd spent some time in Glastonbury, she fell in love with it and decided to stay. Grandma and Grandpa weren't real thrilled about this idea, and they came all the way from Texas to talk some sense into their youngest daughter. Mom even came along. But nobody could change Maggie's mind. Everybody got into a huge argument, and Mom, Grandpa, and Grandma ended up going back to Texas without Maggie, who told them point blank that if they couldn't accept her dedication to the Goddess, then they could just forget about her.

Maggie started a new life, using her given name of Margaret. Before long she got the job at Chalice Well Gardens. Maggie admitted she had wanted to get back in touch with Mom and her parents once she "grew out of her rebellious phase." But so many years had passed by that time, she didn't know how to go about patching things up.

Which was really silly considering how the two of them were going on and on, laughing one minute, crying the next. The crying part got really bad when Mom told Maggie that Grandma had passed away. That made Maggie cry for a long while. Mom made her promise to take a trip back to Texas to see Grandpa as soon as she could manage it. Mom even said we might go along, maybe for Thanksgiving, which sounded pretty good to me.

We'd told Mom everything, but I don't think she really believed us until we showed her the Grail. There was something about it that was undeniably otherworldly. So, when she insisted on coming with us this morning, we couldn't exactly say no.

The garden was even more beautiful in the morning light, so peaceful and serene. None of us spoke, so maybe they all felt that too. It just seemed like a time for quiet. Like we were walking through a church or something.

As we entered the courtyard, I thought about Modred lying at the foot of the steps after Merlin's magic had knocked him out. That seemed like forever ago. So much had happened since then. So much had changed.

We approached the hidden door in the bench. Merlin had assured us that we wouldn't need Excalibur this time, and he was right. After all, there was nothing for magic to protect at the moment. As the lid swung open, Claire and I looked at Mom. She seemed stunned, but excited as we were. We followed Merlin down the ladder, through the tunnel, and into the room where we'd found the Grail.

Merlin motioned at me, so I removed the Grail from the leather pack. I'd left my school backpack in Melora's hut, but I still had the leather pack she'd given me. Although it was obviously part of Avalon, it hadn't disappeared when Avalon did. Maybe because it held the Grail, I don't know. But nothing changed when it no longer held the Grail. I was happy for the souvenir, not that I needed something to remind me about this amazing adventure. I'd never forget this experience.

Mom gasped as I took the Grail out of the tie-dye cloth and its ethereal light filled the room. I handed the cup to Merlin, who whispered something that sounded like a prayer, bowed his head for a moment, then lifted the cup over his head and moved to the center of the room.

He let go of the Grail and it hung there, suspended in air.

We left the Gardens after a long goodbye from Aunt Maggie filled with promises to call soon. She and Mom stood hugging for a good minute before she let her little sister go and climbed into the driver seat of the Renault. Merlin, sitting in the back seat next to me, had a strange look on his face.

"You okay?" I asked him.

"I was just thinking about Vivienne," he said softly, buckling his seatbelt.

My eyebrows shot up. "Right! Now that Morgan's gone—" I said, following his thoughts. "Could the spell be broken?"

"Perhaps we could take a quick detour past the old oaks?" he suggested?

Mom agreed, so she turned left instead of right out of Chalice Gardens and followed Merlin's directions to a road that ran along the opposite side of the Tor than the path we'd taken.

Gog and Magog hardly looked like trees anymore. Only one of the huge oaks was still alive, Merlin said, but honestly, that one didn't look so good either. We wandered around them, but only found some broken picture frames, bags of coins, and old ribbons that might have once been tied around a branch. There was no one finding their way out of a magical trap. No entrance to a secret passageway leading under the Tor. There was nothing out of the ordinary at all.

Merlin sighed. "If Morgan's demise broke the spell, it would have happened yesterday. Vivienne wouldn't have understood where she was or even when she was. She would have been frightened and confused. I should have thought about this sooner. If she did escape the tree, she's not here now." He shook his head and turned back toward the car. We followed him in silence. As we drove off, I stole a glance back at the tree. It stretched grey, dying branches toward the clear blue sky, as if reaching for Heaven. Could Vivienne, the true Lady of the Lake, really still be trapped inside?

As we passed the entrance to the Tor's path, I asked Mom if we could take one last hike up before returning Merlin to his flat and heading back to London. I wanted to see Excalibur one more time.

Local police had cordoned off most of the summit, but it was early enough that nobody official was there. The marker was outside of the yellow tape, and I was shocked nobody noticed there was a big old sword sticking out of it. Its jeweled hilt glittering in the morning light as we approached. "Years ago, I was part of a committee that had this marker placed up here. It's made from the same Welsh stones as a very special stone circle, not too far from here."

"Stonehenge," I breathed, and Merlin nodded.

"Is it stuck in there?" Sydney asked.

Merlin grinned. "Give it a try, my dear."

Sydney stepped up and gave it a try. Excalibur didn't move. Merlin chuckled. "It will remain there, until the time when it is needed again for a holy purpose."

We all touched the jewels on its hilt for good luck, then made our way back down the Tor. When we passed the Living Rock, I paused and let everyone go ahead. I sat for a moment on the bench beside the Rock, running my finger along the words carved into its arm: Forever Avalon. Whoever had carved this here was right. The true Avalon would never die. Morgan's dark realm, on the other hand, was gone. Arthur, and Guinevere, were free.

When I stood up, I saw a small rock lying on the ground at my feet. It was just the right size. I bent down and scooped it up, rubbing my thumb over its rough surface.

With a smile, I slipped it into my pocket.

Weeks later, long after Claire, Mom, and I had returned to London; long after Stanley Doonesbury had met with the ghost writer for Into the Faraway to discuss some "story notes" recently discovered in Fern's flat; long after the first snow had covered the Tor in a blanket of white; Merlin saw Vivienne.

At least, he thought he did.

It was the week before Christmas, and Sydney told me all about it on our regular Saturday night FaceTime. She and Merlin were walking home down High Street after doing some shopping. They'd just rounded the corner onto Sydney's street when Merlin suddenly stopped in the middle of the sidewalk. Sydney said he looked as if he'd seen a ghost. Then he dropped his shopping bags and took off running. This was not an easy thing for him to do, because even though drinking from the Grail had stopped him from aging, it stopped him from aging when he was already a pretty old guy. Running wasn't something he did a lot.

Sydney was so stunned by him taking off like that, she didn't even move. Merlin ran past their flat and toward the Abbey entrance, where he stopped, looking around. By time Sydney caught up to him, he was panting and frustrated. He told her he thought he saw Vivienne near the Abbey Gates. But he'd lost her in a tour group leaving the grounds. He was convinced it was Vivienne though, and insisted they search the Abbey grounds properly.

They didn't find her, of course. But Merlin was sure it was her. Sydney didn't know what to think, but she had a feeling they would be making another trip out to Gog and Magog the next morning.

"So," she said, "did you receive a package today?"

I grinned. "Yup. Did you?"

"I did! In fact, I am off to open it right now. You?"

"Me, too. Think you'll be finished by next weekend?"

"That's the plan." Sydney hesitated. "Wait, please tell me you don't have some outrageous, drawn-out ritual planned for this one."

I had to laugh. "I thought about waiting for the last night of winter break but I just don't think I can do it this time."

"Glad to hear it," Sydney said. "Next week, then. Cheers!"

I picked up the thick envelope and ripped it open.

Inside was an advance copy of Fern Caldwell's final book, Into the Faraway. Doonesbury had clipped a note to the cover.

Merry Christmas, Henderson. Hope it was worth the wait. — D.

I flipped open the cover and thumbed through a couple of pages until I found it. Other than the few of us who knew the truth, the world would think Fern had finished the book before she died. Doonesbury had already hinted to us about the dedication page. He'd said that when we'd disappeared through the doorway that morning, Fern had instructed him about how to finish the final book—including how she wanted him to word the dedication.

Now, as I read her words, my eyes filled with tears, but the smile never left my face.

> *For Sydney, who made it happen.*
> *And for HG, who never gave up ... on me, or on himself.*
> *And, of course, for Arthur!*

Author's Note

Over the past 1500 years, there have been a host of literary accounts about the great King Arthur. The man, who may or may not have even existed, was worshipped by the Celts, became legend across the British Isles, and was romanticized by the French. Many of the stories written or told about Arthur had similar events or qualities that I drew upon to create my own story. In no way should any reader take this account as a study in Arthurian lore, but I do hope I've captured the essence of his legends. Throughout the different stories, spellings of character names and details vary. I chose to use Sir Thomas Malory's version as a base, using his spellings and his accounts of the legend.

Part of what I've always loved about the King Arthur stories is the way they changed depending upon the interests of the time. Into the Faraway is just one way the story could manifest in the 21st century.

This edition, updated more than ten years after the first one, incorporates the technology of today, but the soul of the story remained the same.

Acknowledgements

When it comes to the writing of this book, I did not do it alone. Without the following people and resources, this book would not be what it is, and if truth be told, probably would not be at all. Deepest thanks to:

My first readers: Harrison Smith, Ethan Judd, Katrina Power, Cassidy and MacKenzie Staber, Drew Tucker and Kaylee Geiser. Their enthusiasm and honesty made this a better book. No question.

Jen Judd for her never-ending kindness and steadfast support.

Wendy Mass, the most amazing mentor and editor an aspiring author could ever hope for. Your kindness, encouragement, and generosity were a great gift.

Kevin Mote—who delivered in spades on the cover design. As Henderson would say, Brilliant.

My 2nd grade teacher, Mrs. MacDonald—the first person outside of my family who saw something of note in my crazy stories.

My mother, who raised me with a passion for books and who never stopped believing that someday I would write one of my own.

My father, Roger, who is always there for me with whatever is needed, be that encouragement or a dumb blonde joke.

My amazing boys, Harrison and Benjamin, who gave me the time and enthusiasm to finish, who love me whether the book is good or stinks, and who will be the first ones to tell me if it's the latter. You make everything else in life worth the while.

And my husband, Steve—your unconditional love is what helped me make it through the days when I questioned everything. You were there with a hug and to wipe away the tears of frustration. You believed in the idea for this book so much that you were willing to send me to Glastonbury to uncover it. For that, and for so many other reasons, I love you and thank you with my whole heart.

KIMBERLY J. SMITH
FEBRUARY 2018

Sydney Wakefield: Into the Faraway
by Kimberly J. Smith

Cover design by Kevin Lory Mote

This is a work of fiction. Any resemblance of a character to any
person living or dead is purely coincidental.

Montage Books for Children